Out of Bounds

by

Melissa Klein

Out of Uniform Series

Out of Bounds

Cover Art by *Angela Anderson*

The Wild Rose Press, Inc.
PO Box 708
Adams Basin, NY 14410-0708
Visit us at www.thewildrosepress.com

Publishing History
First Champagne Rose Edition, 2016
Print ISBN 978-1-5092-1088-6
Digital ISBN 978-1-5092-1089-3

Out of Uniform Series
Published in the United States of America

He nodded as if they'd settled the matter.
"Friends then?"

Avery looked at the rugged hand he offered, wondering what it would feel like against her skin. "Okay." She extended her hand and found out. The warmth sent small tremors through her body, building pockets of desire in places she hadn't felt physical need in years. Her breath caught.

Connor tugged on the hand he held in his, focusing her attention on him, then with his other he fingered one of her curls that had come loose from her ponytail. "How is it possible you've gotten more beautiful?"

Pulling out of a 5G dive was easier than pulling out of his grasp, especially with the urge to sink into his arms so strong. Avery dug deep and snatched her hand from his. "I don't think this is a good idea," she said, though at the moment she'd have trouble saying specifically what was wrong with letting him continue to brush his thumb across her cheek.

Connor shrugged. "Maybe not. But it doesn't mean we won't have fun doing it."

Being with him would be like putting her plane in a dive—exhilarating as hell and just as dangerous. She should send him on his merry way with a couple well-placed sharp words.

His offer dangled tantalizingly in the air between them.

She wanted Connor. There was no sense in lying to herself about that. She also wanted a twenty-pound box of chocolate. In the long run, neither would be good for her.

Dedication

I dedicate this book to women in uniform
and the memory of Lieutenant Colonel Jimmie Mims,
my great, great aunt,
who served her country during World War II

Chapter One

Avery Madigan shimmied, trying to get her pantyhose up her hips. She'd planned on having enough time to change in her hotel room instead of the microscopic restroom she'd found at the far end of the hangar. *What was it Murphy said about plans?* Since zero-six hundred not one person, animal, or inanimate object had cooperated with her. "Why should my underwear be any different?" she muttered under her breath.

"Get the lead out, Mad Dog," David Collins said, using her navy call sign. "They've started without you." Three years after she'd left active duty, her former wingman still had her back.

Except, he couldn't help with her dress whites which had shrunk a bit since the last time she'd put them on. "I'm well aware of the situation, Opie. I don't need a status update," she replied through the bathroom door.

Avery never ran late, didn't do the last minute rush thing. She drew in a breath as she silently cursed her ex-husband, Rob. Next time she should probably calculate a larger window for him to pick up their son instead of the one hour she'd allowed this morning. After tugging the skirt down and cramming her feet into the butt-ugly shoes that went with the uniform, she snatched open the door to the head. Only the opportunity to pay homage to her mentor could prompt her to return to this part of coastal North Carolina—the place where her military career stalled and her marriage went down in flames.

David eyed her from stem to stern. "You clean up good."

She rolled her eyes. "If that's supposed to be a compliment, I don't see how you convinced Stephanie to marry you." Then as she stalked past him, she called over her shoulder, "If you're waiting on me, you're backing up."

She pushed through the double doors leading to the hangar just as her name was announced. "Lieutenant Commander Avery Elizabeth Madigan, U.S. Naval Reserves, arriving."

Following the whistle that piped her aboard, she walked through the honor guard.

Military ceremonies were as much a part of her growing up as horseback riding and Girl Scouts. Still, she preferred sitting in the audience as she had when her father had been in the army rather than actively participating. Avery kept her gaze straight ahead, ignoring the impressive crowd who'd come to honor a former commanding officer as he retired.

Admiral Griffin opened the throttle on his retirement ceremony, even opting for rituals that didn't translate well from the ships where they originated to aircraft hangars. He cocked an eyebrow as she took her seat, causing a knot in her stomach. She'd rather ditch her plane in the drink than disappoint the Old Man. Not much beyond her six-year-old son, Will, managed to tap into the emotions she kept guarded beneath a tough exterior.

Going through the motions of saluting the flag and sitting through the chaplain's invocation, Avery's mind wandered to the past couple of years. God only knew how she'd have coped during her divorce if it hadn't been for her navy family.

Her name was called again, and she pushed aside the numerous distractions vying for her attention. Will's trip to Florida with his father and the career-shaping meeting she had at the end of the week could all wait. Right now, she needed to focus on the twenty-minute speech she committed to memory. "Admiral Griffin leaves the navy with a legacy of honor, courage, and leadership," she began.

She executed her speech flawlessly until she made the mistake of taking her eyes off David and Stephanie who were seated in the back row. There he sat, second-row center, the devil who'd plagued her for the past twenty years. Lt. Commander Connor St. James, call sign Titan, probably bribed someone into giving him a place with the dignitaries attending the ceremony. Dressed in a black suit that complemented his dark hair and blue eyes, he looked as comfortable seated between Senator Tallmadge and General Switzer as he had sitting in the cockpit of his Super Hornet. Even the goatee he'd grown since leaving the navy looked good on him. Connor smiled up at her like he was her greatest supporter rather than her greatest rival.

Her attention faltered as his smile broadened into a devilish grin. Heat bloomed in her belly, sending tendrils of electricity through her veins. She broke eye contact. Darn him. He'd always been able to do that, make her lose focus.

She glanced at her notes. "After serving in Desert

3

Storm, Admiral Griffin returned to the States…" For the remainder of her speech she managed not to stumble again. "On behalf of those who had the privilege of serving under you, we wish you fair winds and following seas."

Returning to her seat, her shoulders relaxed for the first time in months. Between her civilian job, the Reserves, and being a single mom, she'd been running off her feet. Now she could enjoy the Admiral's reception later and a few days of long overdue vacation.

"During the First Gulf War," Admiral Griffin said, recalling his time serving under Fleet Admiral Carter.

Avery tuned into her mentor's reminisces—some men entered your life and made it better. Her eyes gravitated to Connor—while others barged in and screwed things up. He was at the top of that particular list, and that was saying something considering she had an ex who'd screwed half the women at her last post.

Titan had been under the admiral's command same as she. But, she'd known him much longer than that, over twenty years now. The sorry rascal grew more handsome every year. The dark suit gave him a distinguished look as much as the cocky smile on his face made him look like the scoundrel he was. He winked at her, having caught her staring. He knew he was good looking, too. Avery clenched her fists. *Dammit.* He couldn't fool her with his wicked smile, not anymore. Experience taught her some hard lessons, but once learned she used them like a Kevlar vest.

****

Connor shook the older gentleman's doughy hand again. "Pleasure to meet you, Senator," he said over the din of military music playing in the background. As

4

soon as the ceremony was over and he'd paid his respects to Admiral and Mrs. Griffin, Connor kicked it into gear. He should have taken a seat with the other men and women who'd served under the admiral. As much as he would have enjoyed reconnecting with the guys, at the moment he had more pressing matters.

"Likewise, Commander. Your take on our military budget gives me food for thought," the senior statesman said.

Connor worked his way through the crowd of movers and shakers of not only his home state of North Carolina but the whole country. The key to holding your own in a place you didn't belong was to look as if you did. His glad-handing had nothing to do with massaging his ego. The only way to keep his family's business open after his older brother's gross mismanagement was by making connections with these bigwigs. While Stephen, the heir to the St. James empire, had seen Aviation Options as his personal piggy bank, it fell to Connor to pull the once-thriving business out of the toilet.

His mind flashed to the disaster of embezzlement and crushing debt his brother had left. Connor vowed to pull the company out of near bankruptcy—that was if he could keep his mind on networking the crowd and off the redhead standing in the middle of a crowd of admirers.

Even as he talked to General Hammond about the situation in Syria and listened while a congresswoman told a story about growing up on a tobacco farm, his gaze followed Avery around the room. He remembered the day a little over three years ago when he'd last seen her because it was also the day the rudder came off his life plans. After that he'd put in for the discharge he wasn't ready to take.

God, I miss the navy.

As a young boy in LaGrange, dreams of escaping the shadow of his older brother and the yolk of expectation the St. James name carried in that small North Carolina town fueled his actions. He'd done everything from getting top grades to earning his Eagle Scout rank in order to make it into the Naval Academy. Not that he was a choirboy by any stretch of the imagination. There wasn't a risk he hadn't taken or rule he hadn't broken. He knew even as a kid that if he wanted to get ahead, he had to play out of bounds—which was the reason he and Avery got along about as well as wind shear and an ultralight. Other than that time during their first year at the Academy, she'd been the poster girl for the navy. No breaking curfew, no sneaking beers, and definitely no fraternization with the other plebes for his girl.

He tracked her movement as she spoke to a two-star. As General Madigan's daughter, Avery's career was preordained. He'd bet money on her making captain before retirement. Much as he would like to say she rode her daddy's coattails, outside of his own skills behind the stick, he knew of no one who was better at flying the Super Hornet. No one filled out a uniform better either. Pretty even as a twelve-year-old with braids and braces, over the past twenty years she'd matured into a beauty that had nothing to do with Botox and liposuction. Confidence was its own beauty cream.

A familiar and important face stepped into his field of vision, the only thing that could distract him from watching the woman who'd harried his thoughts and haunted his dreams since middle school. Charles Hendricks was a vice president with Louisiana Gas and Oil. Getting a contract to move their guys back and forth to their oil rigs in the Gulf would be a boon to Aviation Options. Even if he managed to reel in the contract with LGO, Connor wasn't going to be satisfied until he had a nice, thick cushion of profit to keep the family business well into the black. With not only his extended family but thirty employees dependent on the company, he had a lot weighing on his success.

His phone vibrated on his hip. He checked the screen—Sofia's school. In addition to taking on the job of running the family business after his older brother's suicide, he was now responsible for his fifteen-year-old niece. *God, and he thought the Gulf War had been tough.*

"Connor St. James," he announced, holding his breath for the latest round of bad news from LaGrange High.

"Mr. St. James, I'm calling to let you know Sofia is absent from classes today."

Connor massaged the bridge of his nose. Well, it wasn't because he hadn't taken her there. Before heading down to River Bend Naval Air Station, he'd hand delivered her to the campus for the last day of class before Spring Break. "Yes, I know," he fibbed. "She wasn't feeling well, so I thought it best she stay home this morning."

Connor arranged for her to spend the time with a friend's family, one he knew would keep an eye on the girls while business took him south to Wilmington. It looked like Sofia planned to start her break a little early. He ended the call and headed in the direction of his car. If he had to drive the ten miles back to LaGrange, he'd miss the meeting with Carolina Entertainment. Running his hand through his hair with one hand, he dialed her cell phone with the other. Winning the contract to fly musicians and actors around the South played a major role in keeping his company afloat. God, he hoped he could work this out over the phone.

"Why aren't you in school?" he asked by way of greeting. This wasn't the first time she'd ditched class, and even if he'd have done the same at her age, he wasn't letting her get away with stuff like that.

"I started my period," she answered in a teary voice. "By the time I realized it, I'd stained my clothes."

Connor's face heated. Functions of the female body topped the list of things he was unprepared and unqualified to handle. Shoving aside his embarrassment in favor of more urgent concerns, he asked, "Where are you now?" The high school was two miles from home, and the only thing more worrying than her walking the distance was her catching a ride with some eighteen-year-old boy who was also ditching class.

"I'm home. I called Meghan's mother. She's waiting on me while I change then she'll take me back to school."

Sofia's explanation sounded a little too tidy for his liking—not because he had developed a parent's ear for bull, but because it sounded like the type of yarn he'd have woven to tell his parents. Plus, she'd just last week lied to him about being at the library studying.

"Put Meghan's mom on the phone." After a huff that let him know she was once again aggravated with him, he ascertained that indeed his niece's story was true. "Thank you, Mrs. Barnes; you don't know how grateful I am for your help. Please let me talk to Sofia again."

When she came back on the line his one goal was to smooth things over with her. As much as the past few years had been hard on him, it was nothing compared to what his niece had endured. "You handled yourself well, Little Bit," he said, using her pet name. "Call me if you need anything." As long as it didn't involve personal care items. "I love you, and I'll see you Sunday."

With the latest crisis handled, Connor double-timed it through the parking lot. He had less than an hour until his meeting with Carolina Entertainment and too much was riding on it to risk something like a flat or traffic to get in the way. He was just reaching for the SUV's handle when he heard his name.

"Titan."

Connor turned to see Sabastian Baron, one of his old squad members, headed his way. The guy was dressed in a dark suit similar to Connor's, and like him, had left active duty. "Bash, how's the world treating you, my man?" he asked, wondering if the rumors were true that he'd transitioned his aviation skills into a career as a military-thriller novelist.

"Like a baby treats a diaper," his former naval flight officer answered, with a grin. "I tried to get a minute with you, but every time I caught sight you were schmoozing with the brass."

Connor shrugged. "You know how it is, got to make a living. What's doing with you?"

"Not much. I wanted to invite you to Wayfarer's

tonight. The squad's getting together over there to knock back a few and pretend we're still the shit."

"What time?" God, it had been a coon's age since he'd seen the guys, or done something that wasn't related to taking care of either business or Sofia.

"Eight o'clock," Bash answered.

That would work. After he finished his meeting, he'd still have time to take care of a few things at Wrightsville Marina. "I'll see you there," he said, wondering if Avery would skip the after party.

Chapter Two

"Remind me again why I play pool with you, Mad Dog," Bash said, running his hand through his hair.

After the admiral's retirement party, Avery and several of the guys took their celebration on the road. They ended up at Wayfarer's, a bar about a mile from the hotel where she was staying. For all her day had started off badly, it was definitely ending on an upswing. One more shot and she would have run the table and relieved Bash of the twenty bucks he bet against her.

"You're a glutton for punishment?" she asked over her shoulder where he, Opie, and Hank nursed drinks along with their wounded male pride. The ball sank into the pocket with a pleasant thunk as it landed on top of one of its friends.

Instead of gloating, she put down her cue. "I'll be right back. The next round's on me, guys," she said, walking toward the head.

After taking care of business, she was washing up when Opie's wife entered. "There you are," Stephanie said. The petite brunette leaned against the wall, watching Avery as she used a wet paper towel to repair her makeup. "Ready to have some fun this week?"

She let out a sigh. "Yes, between work and Rob nearly making me late for the admiral's ceremony, I seriously need to unwind."

"We'll make that our mission then," Stephanie said, grasping her hand on their way out of the restroom.

Opie, Stephanie, and their two kids were staying at the same hotel as Avery. The two women planned to hang out by the pool and take advantage of some of the hotel's spa amenities. No doubt Stephanie would make it her top priority to see to it that Avery relaxed. In fact, it seemed as if the woman planned on starting the cruise-director routine right then. Stephanie touched her arm when she headed toward the pool tables. "Come hang out with me. Competing with David and the guys won't help you relax."

Stephanie had a point. As much fun as kicking back with her former squad members was, her competitive streak couldn't let it go when she missed a shot or one of the guys started ribbing her.

Soon after she slid into the booth across from Stephanie, a waitress moved in to take their orders. "What can I get you?"

Avery had been knocking back diet sodas in the other room, but maybe a glass of wine would help loosen the screw in her back. "A glass of your house white, please."

Stephanie took a sip from her glass. "Are you and Will still coming to our place for the Fourth?"

Independence Day at the Collin's house was a tradition that withstood the test of distance, deployment, and even her divorce from Rob. Her stomach twisted a bit. This year would be a little different. Avery shook her head. "It'll just be me. Rob asked if he could have Will."

Stephanie arched an eyebrow but held back a

comment as the waitress set down their drinks.

After she left, Avery explained. "He's been pretty consistent with visitation in the last several months." She played with her glass of wine, swirling the liquid around in the glass.

"That's good to hear," Stephanie said, patting her hand.

Letting go of the bitterness against her ex-husband was a work in progress. Three years ago, she returned from a six-month deployment in the Gulf to find out how well Rob had been doing his part as a military spouse. Husbands and wives of officers had an unpaid and underappreciated duty to the enlisted personnel's family. Stephanie was a whiz at the job, checking in with the families in David's crew, offering help with finding childcare, negotiating dependent benefits, or providing a listening ear.

Rob had taken on the duty in another way, one that involved him "servicing" the wives of several shipmates. In addition to the pain of betrayal, her skipper saw it as a failure on her part. Rob had taken off a week after she'd returned. She and Will hadn't heard anything from him for months after that.

Not knowing where Rob was made it impossible for her to finalize their divorce—and kept her and Will in a state of limbo that hadn't been good for either of them. Now they were on the flip side of that period in their life, she was ready for some smooth air.

Stephanie must have tuned into that thought because she touched on a subject she'd been pondering herself. "There's a guy in our neighborhood I'd like you to meet. He's in his late thirties, a widower with two girls in middle school—"

Stephanie was the closest thing she had to a best friend, which meant Avery had no problem cutting her off. "The last thing I need right now—" She began before her phone went off in her purse. The UFO-like noise identified the caller as her boss. "I need to get this," she said, snagging the phone while sliding out of the booth.

"Did you send that proposal over to Carolina Entertainment?"

"Yes, Douglas." She struggled to keep the impatience out of her voice. She'd been working on the project for the past several weeks. It wasn't likely she'd forget such an important piece of Flight Innovations' bid. "And I confirmed my appointment with the vice president for Friday at four."

Avery chewed her thumb, waiting for her boss' response. Several heartbeats of weighted silence passed. "I'm still not convinced this is the direction we need to be taking the company."

"I know." Boy, did she know. The man never missed an opportunity to tell her what he thought of her ideas. She was spot-on about pursuing this business. Expanding Flight Innovations' core services would increase their profit. "With the company acquiring Jet South's assets, we now have the passenger planes we need without having to invest money in new equipment." Why the hell the guy couldn't see that was beyond her. Probably because he didn't want to listen to anything she had to say.

Avery made two vertical moves in the year and a half she'd been at Flight Innovations. Perhaps the old fart was worried she was after his job. She wasn't. She was after his boss' job. "Everything's under control.

I've got a great presentation and a solid bid. I don't think we can lose."

More silence on his end.

A throb began behind her eyes. "Leave it to me, Douglas." Some sixth sense told her not only her promotion depended on her closing the deal but that her job was riding on it. "I'll talk to you after the meeting."

After hanging up, she returned to the booth. "Sorry. That was the boss." She kept the phone out. He usually followed phone calls with a series of emails as he thought of more points he wanted to make. On cue her phone dinged again. She turned it to read the message. *You've got one chance to make this work.*

"God, I need these few days off."

Stephanie finished off her drink as the waitress set another in front of her. "Girl, you need to get laid." That from Mrs. Happily Married. She and Opie were the poster children for love everlasting.

"You might be right." Avery hadn't had sex with anyone but herself since she and Rob split. The problem standing in her way was she didn't think she'd ever trust a man enough to get married again. Some companionship wouldn't be a bad thing—of the no-long-term-expectations variety.

She scanned the bar. She'd been a lowly ensign the last time she'd been in a bar looking for a hook up. She hadn't enjoyed it back then, and going by the men in this particular establishment, things hadn't improved in the past few years. Where were all the nice, single, straight men?

"How about this one?" Stephanie asked, nodding discreetly at the guy headed in their direction.

Wearing a tight T-shirt and board shorts, and

sporting the artfully messy hair she'd seen on cologne adds, he leaned in a little too close as he asked, "Can I buy you ladies a drink?"

Stephanie grinned. "I'm good, but you can buy one for Avery here."

She wasn't so taken with the guy's aren't-I-something-else routine. "No thanks," she corrected. She probably had underwear older than him.

The Ian Somerhalder wannabe moved on with a shrug.

Stephanie swatted at Avery. "He was into you. I could tell."

"Please." She rolled her eyes. "I probably reminded him of a babysitter he once had a crush on."

Never one to dwell on defeat, Stephanie motioned to the front of the bar. "Well, if you won't let me fix you up, at least come do karaoke with me. We haven't done that since that time in Pensacola."

God, that had been fun. Probably the last time Avery had felt free, like anything was possible. Instead of the survival mode she'd been in for the past few years. "Let's do it," she said. "But I get to pick the song. I'm not singing 'Save a Horse, Ride a Cowboy' like we did last time."

****

Connor propped his pool cue against his shoulder and took a long pull on his beer. "Who else is here?"

"Just us," Bash answered, pointing to the four guys watching Connor and him play a round of Nine Ball. "Dice left with someone about an hour ago, and Pappy couldn't get a kitchen pass." He took a swig from his long neck. "Why?"

Connor shrugged. "No reason. Just making polite

conversation."

The corner of Bash's mouth turned up. "Yeah, right." He jerked his chin in the direction of the other room. "She's in the bar with Stephanie."

No need to say who *she* was. Their rivalry was legendary. Connor craned to see inside Wayfarer's main bar area and caught a glimpse of Avery at a booth with Opie's wife. He tamped down on the urge to step closer to get a better look. He shouldn't have been so keen to see her again. The last thing he needed was to go twenty rounds with She Whose Hair Matched Her Temperament.

They'd first met back when they were kids. Her dad was stationed at the base not far from LaGrange, and for a couple years she and Connor attended the same middle school. Then her hair had been a bright red.

"You playing or staring at her?" Bash asked, jerking Connor from his thoughts.

"I was looking for the waitress," he said as he held up his drink. "I could use another beer." He'd actually been thinking how Avery's hair had darkened over the years to a deep auburn. Noting the change and wondering if it denoted a mellowing in the woman's famous temper wasn't why he'd come. After this afternoon, he'd earned a little down time. His meeting with Carolina Entertainment had gone well, but between it and Sofia's little drama, he was looking forward to a few days on his boat.

Connor set his empty on the ledge ringing the room, then approached the table and lined up his shot. There was a place to fly by the seat of his pants, executing a perfect carrier landing, and pool wasn't it.

The four ball sank in the corner pocket and over the next few minutes he proceeded to run the table.

"I just can't catch a break tonight," Bash told him, fishing in his wallet.

Connor pocketed the twenty. The win should have felt better. "What say I give you a chance to earn it back?" He gestured toward the table with his chin. "I can't send you home in defeat."

Bash flashed a grin. "You're on."

As Connor waited for him to rack the balls for the next game, he rubbed the back of his neck. Then he paced the room, making sure to steer away from the view into the other room. He was supposed to be celebrating with old friends, not looking for trouble. But, damn, a distraction of the female variety wouldn't be amiss. Waiting to hear from Carolina Entertainment would be crazy-making if he didn't channel his thoughts elsewhere.

His sales pitch had been spot on, and he'd answered every one of the guy's concerns about choosing a smaller charter company. That's all he could do. But losing to one of the other air transport companies wasn't an option. Over the course of the contract, it'd be a steady source of revenue for Aviation Options. Connor's mind swam with numbers, both black and red. He'd give his left nut to find out what Flight Innovations' proposal looked like. If he could, he'd make damn sure his was better. Carolina Entertainment was taking bids until close of business on Friday, and nothing said Connor couldn't sweeten the deal if he needed to. The livelihood of Aviation Options depended on him winning that contract. The alternative meant selling his beloved boat.

He'd had a few of offers to buy her over the years but clung to the hope he could turn the family business around without sacrificing the last reminder of his former life. Just thinking about parting with *The Nemesis* put a knot in his gut. Over the past three years he'd sold off everything he owned. First, to cover the loans Stephen took out, then to keep the company afloat while Connor worked on getting new contracts.

Back when things had first gone south on him, he'd entertained the idea of just taking Sofia and letting the family business implode. One look at the faces of the people who'd lose their jobs and he'd tossed that option overboard. There was another reason he couldn't walk away. Proving to his old man that he wasn't the screw up came in a close second. Damn, to be thirty-two and still seeking his deceased father's approval. Way to be a second son stereotype. Stephen had been the heir, while Connor was the spare.

The opening notes of a popular rock anthem drifted into the room. "Oh shit, those two are at it again," Opie said, slamming his beer down on one of the tall tables dotting the room.

"What?" Hank Taggart asked.

"Oh man, check it." Bash threw his head back with a laugh. "Stephanie and Mad need to take that show on the road."

Opie body-blocked the doorway leading to the bar area. "I'll pay you guys to stay in here. They don't need any encouragement."

Hank pushed Opie aside, and the other guys abandoned their bullshit and pool. Connor followed them into Wayfarer's main room, interested in anything to keep his mind off his old family issues. Especially if

Avery was part of the distraction. Whether she was flying, tearing someone a new one, or giving a heartfelt speech, she never failed to enthrall him.

On the far side of the stage, Stephanie and Avery stood behind a Karaoke machine with mics in their hands. Now this was something he hadn't seen her do.

"Those two get up to more mischief," Opie said, shaking his head. "It's a good thing we're not neighbors anymore." After a minute of pacing while scrubbing his hands through his short hair, Opie gave up and plopped down at a nearby table.

Far from making fools of themselves, the women were drawing attention of the admiring kind. People were holding up their lit cell phones the way kids back in his concert days held up their Bics. With their arms wrapped around each other, they were quite the pair. Stephanie had a nice soprano voice that rang clear. Then there was Avery's alto.

Her sultry sound went straight to his cock. Deep and throaty, she sounded like she was making love as she sang the lyrics. She poured everything into her performance, closing her eyes and belting out the lyrics as if she were singing to a crowd of adoring fans.

When their duet ended, Avery started up her solo act, singing a romantic ballad. *Damn, he didn't know she had it in her.* She sang as if she was alone and the lyrics were from a deep part of her soul. He should have known she'd have a fabulous voice. She approached everything she did with an eye toward mastery and made it look so goddamned easy as she did it.

Connor shook his head, a combination of surprised admiration at yet another example of Avery's lengthy skill set and a reminder that wanting and getting were two different things. He wasn't any more likely to win anything other than her sharp tongue than he was getting his old man's approval. But that didn't stop him from appreciating the way she sang, flew a plane, or filled out her jeans.

When the song came to an end, Opie bolted for the stage. "I got to get Steph off of there, or she'll get ideas about being on *You've Got Talent* again."

"Oh, come on, Opie. Don't spoil their fun," Connor called. He wasn't done watching Mad Dog show her wilder side.

Stephanie leaped into Opie's arms, letting him carry her from the stage in an over the top display of what a happy marriage should look like. Not that Connor knew anything about functional relationships. The two up-close-and-personal marriages he'd seen had been enough of a disaster to convince him happily ever after only existed in the movies. As Opie set his wife on her feet, she staggered a bit as if she'd had more than a couple drinks before taking to the stage.

Was that what Avery had used to get up the nerve to put on the performance? The woman he'd known since childhood was too squared away to let loose in front of a crowd of half-drunk sailors. She put out a hand, grabbing the back of a booth as she made her way back to the table. Yep. She had a couple drinks in her. Maybe more than a couple given the way she used the backs of the booths to guide her way.

Avery was still laughing as she headed to a booth. Then she stumbled as she reached across the table for her purse. Surely she didn't plan to drive like that. Not stopping to investigate the reason behind the sudden protective instinct or to remind himself that she wasn't his problem, he followed her out to the parking lot.

****

Riding high from her and Stephanie's performance, Avery followed her friends outside. A few days with them was exactly the catharsis she needed. Stephanie's laughter carried across the night then died as she and Opie stopped by their car to kiss. She rolled her eyes at the only downside to vacationing with Mr. and Mrs. Forever.

She picked her way across the parking lot. The half glass of wine she drank over an hour ago had nothing to do with the reason she was toddling like a recruit who hadn't gotten her sea legs under her. The stilettos were responsible. The sore feet and aching side from laughing so much were well worth the pain. For those few minutes on stage she wasn't Lt. Commander Madigan, the Director of Sales and Marketing at Flight Innovations, or even Mom. She was Avery, a still youngish woman who enjoyed a good rock anthem. Well, she still felt young even if she could see her twenties in the rearview mirror.

In the semidarkness she stumbled over some unseen obstacle. "Damn," she cursed as she reached inside her purse for a flashlight. Maybe the shoes hadn't been such a good idea, even if they did make her legs look long. The sound of footsteps behind her had her picking up the pace and reaching for the mace instead of the light.

This was exactly why she didn't drink. Intoxicated women put themselves at risk. Back on active duty while her squad had cut loose in bars all over the world, she always acted as designated driver. Mother Mad, they called her. A male who had a few too many might wake up to find he'd been rolled by a mugger. A female could awaken to much worse.

"Mad Dog, hold up."

The baritone voice burned through the remains of her afterglow. *Great.* Just what she needed to kill her good mood—Connor St. James. Although, there was nothing saintly about the guy.

In those four words, time compressed and she was back at the Academy. They'd been friends then, but it had been years since they had a civil word for each other. She still wasn't interested in talking to him. "Stupid stillies." She growled as something caught in her shoe.

In the seconds it took her to work out the pebble, Connor caught up to her. "What do you think you're doing?" he asked, grabbing her elbow. His touch sent a charge of electricity up her arm.

On instinct, she wrenched out of his grasp. "What's it look like, Titan? I'm leaving."

He reached for her, taking her by the shoulders and pulling her in close. "Not like this, you're not. Give me your keys."

Twin emotions fought for dominance—anger that he thought she'd risk her life, as well as the lives of other people on the road, and frustration at herself for reacting to his touch. It heated her entire body the way her speech that morning or her performance a few minutes ago never could. For the moment, the first emotion won out. "I'm not drunk," she said, pushing against the hard plane of his chest. As she shoved away, she stumbled again.

"Yeah, right. Now give me your keys." His full lips thinned to form a straight line. Beneath the boyish charm lay a man who wasn't going to easily let her get away.

Suddenly, not only was walking a problem so was breathing. "It's my shoes," she said, her words coming out breathy. "I'm not used to heels." The three-inch sandals she'd worn to the bar topped her off at just under six feet. She still needed to tilt her chin to meet his gaze. "You want to take me back inside and have me use the Breathalyzer?" she asked, daring him to do it. He might be messing with her head with his whole concerned friend routine, but she wasn't letting him know that.

A couple heartbeats of silence passed as his gaze raked over her. "No, I believe you." He closed the distance, a smile playing at his lips. "Although, I can't believe that was you up there on the stage."

Avery jutted out her chin. She wasn't a stick in the mud. Not all the time, anyway. "What? You don't think I can have fun?"

The corner of his mouth turned up. "Yes, actually, I know you can." He touched a piece of her hair. "I thought you'd forgotten how."

"I haven't." She brushed his hand aside and moved toward her car. "I'm on vacation," she explained, although she didn't owe him one.

His full lips curved up in an arrogant smile the semidarkness couldn't hide. Between the spark in his blue eyes and the goatee, Connor looked like the devil himself. "Good for you."

She hit the key fob as she resumed her trajectory to her car.

"Slow down a minute, Mad. I want to hear how you've been," he called after her.

Avery shot him a look over her shoulder. "No. You don't."

His long legs chewed up the distance between them, catching her before she had a chance to get inside her car. "We don't have to be enemies, you know. Our rivalry will die if we stop feeding it." Connor caged her against her car with his arms.

Enemies was too strong a word. It suggested hatred. In that moment with him so near she could see flecks of green in his blue eyes, her body screamed a different emotion. "What do you think you're doing?" she asked, narrowing her eyes.

"This," he said, tilting her chin and capturing her mouth with his. His lips were gentle, seeking rather than demanding. They moved like velvet over hers, reminding her of times before he'd shown himself as a man who'd stop at nothing to win.

The past was as lost to them as the size four jeans she was never getting back into and her faith in the goodness of man. She jerked her mouth away. "What is it with you?" This wasn't the only time he'd stolen a kiss from her. The first time they'd been twelve and prompted by her announcement her father had been transferred to a new post.

Connor smiled but didn't step away. "Beats the hell out of me," he said looking as surprised by the kiss as she.

Avery swiped her mouth with the back of her hand. "Well, stop it." Her heart pounded in her chest. In that simple meeting of lips, her entire body had responded. Her nipples peaked and desire pooled in her belly. Which was a bad idea on so many levels. "I don't need—"

25

He tilted her chin. "Yeah, I think you do."

Avery turned her back to him so he couldn't see how much the kiss affected her. Or his words. "Maybe I do, but you're the last person I'd want to do it with."

Stephanie might have been right about her needing to find someone, but Connor wasn't the one. In fact, of all the people she could hook up with, he was the exact wrong person. "Now move it before I knee you where it counts," she said, hiding her vulnerability with anger.

His eyes widened. "Good to know you're still the same, Mad Dog," he said with a chuckle. "It was real nice catching up." He backed away, letting her inside her rental car.

Connor strolled back to the bar, but she couldn't muster the will to move. Hitting the door locks, she prayed he hadn't sensed how aroused she'd been by his kiss. She managed after two tries to get the key in the ignition. As she pointed the Prius toward her beachside hotel, she could still feel his lips against hers despite her childish attempt to wipe the sensation away.

Chapter Three

The next morning, Avery's thighs burned as she ran along the beach. Staying outside of the surf, her bare toes fought to gain purchase in the sand. The coarse granules were murder on her freshly painted pedicure but were giving her workout the extra kick it needed. When she reached the halfway mark she stopped to check her time. Six minutes, twenty-five seconds, not bad for a mile. Turning back to the hotel, she made a wager with herself. If she could get mile two down to six-twenty she'd have a chocolate muffin instead of the usual oat bran breakfast.

With the memories of last night's karaoke still fresh in her mind, she made another promise to herself. She'd do more fun things like that and spend less time being the stick in the mud she'd become. Her vacation was the perfect time to begin her resolution.

Although, now that her mind replayed the previous evening, the last part of her evening wasn't as relaxing as the beginning. Nothing about Titan lent itself to calm and peaceful. Over the years, he'd honed his talent for getting under her skin to damned near an art form. What prompted him to kiss her? She did know what went through his mind right afterward. That wide-eyed look said he was thinking of the first time he'd stolen a kiss. While she'd gotten her temper under control and was no longer prone to letting her fists do her talking, she'd taken more than a little glee at the fear in his eyes. Reaching her beachfront hotel, she couldn't suppress the smile tugging at the corners of her mouth. She had to give Connor one thing: he wasn't a man she'd ever forget.

After noting her time and seeing she'd met her goal, she paused to catch her breath. With palms pressed to her thighs, she drew in the sea air. No air freshener in the world could capture that scent. Waves crashing against the shore mixed with the cry of sea gulls to create a lullaby that damned sleep machine she'd bought couldn't replicate either. Tension eased from her body. Funny considering she had never much enjoyed the beach.

A single boat that hadn't been there when she checked in yesterday was docked at the marina. With the early morning light illuminating it, the sleek yacht captured her attention. Though she'd spent years in the navy as an aviator, she wasn't as familiar with ocean-going vessels as airplanes. She could however appreciate beauty even if she didn't know how long it was or how fast it could go. It called to mind lazy days spent sunning on its deck.

Then the view got even better. The dark outline of a man emerged from below deck. Her feet rooted to the sand like stubborn sea grass as the tall, silhouetted figure stretched in the morning light. Though he was a few yards from her, looks that strong and masculine translated well over distance. She wouldn't mind spending a few days with that type of man. Maybe he'd come ashore later. But if she'd didn't get a move on, she'd still be inside slaving away on her laptop.

Avery reached for the key card she'd tucked in the

pocket of her gym shorts and was opening her hotel room when her ring tone chimed. As she stepped in, it stopped and the message dumped into her mailbox before she could pick up her phone. She didn't need to check the caller ID to know who it was. Her boss liked to keep her on a short leash, and no doubt after finishing his first cup of coffee, he'd come up with half a dozen or so questions to throw at her.

"You can wait until I've had my shower," she told the phone. Flight Innovations hadn't imploded overnight, and if any of their planes had gone down she would have heard it on the morning news. Everything else could wait fifteen minutes. Her vacation had officially started, and Avery was on beach time.

****

After enjoying the sunrise and a mug of hot coffee topside, Connor returned below deck. He had a few minor repairs to finish so he and Sofia could take *The Nemesis* out when school ended at the end of May. If he didn't have to sell her before then. In the meantime, he planned to enjoy every minute of the next few days.

Connor slid his hand further down the handle of the crescent wrench, trying to increase the torque. "Come on," he begged. "Give it up." The bolt refused to submit. Instead, it was his grip that gave way, the bolt biting into his hand as the wrench slipped from his grasp. "Son of a…!" Those might have been the words that flew out of his mouth, but the ones he'd been thinking were far less G-rated. He continued with the stream of mild-mannered expletives as he reached for a clean rag to stem the flow of blood.

Since taking on parenting duties, he'd been trying to clean up his language. Even though Sofia heard foul language at school, he wanted to set an example for the fifteen-year-old who'd had little in the way of moral compasses in her life.

After bandaging his hand, he got back to work on repairing the boat's engine. It looked as if she needed new valves and gaskets in addition to the work he'd already completed that morning. "Crap, I need to go ashore." The repairs proved to be nearly as exasperating as his niece when she was in one of her teenaged angst moods. Connor smiled to himself. He and his niece were quite an unlikely pair and too much alike for their own good.

He went topside after snagging his wallet and the keys to his truck. The sun glinting off the water tempted him. He loved the water almost as much as he did flying. If he didn't need to run errands, he'd have dived in for a swim. His family's trips to North Carolina's Outer Banks had been the inspiration for joining the navy.

He hoofed it across the sand. Twenty feet ahead lay another female who also pleasured in making his life more interesting than he'd like. The logical part of his brain, the one that said he had enough on his plate today, suggested he keep walking. After all, she had her nose in a book and hadn't seen him. The other part of him, the one that had been getting him into trouble since way before he was Sofia's age, drew him to Avery like Icarus soaring too close to the sun. Nothing good would come of the folly, but he'd sure as fuck enjoy the flight while it lasted.

****

Despite warmth from the late-morning sun, goose bumps suddenly danced along Avery's skin. She could sense curious eyes on her as surely as she could tell when Will was doing something he shouldn't. These eyes weren't checking the cover of her book trying to see if she was reading that erotic best seller. This interest had a little heat of its own behind it. She squirmed under the scrutiny. Maybe it was that gorgeous male she'd seen on the yacht this morning.

When a cool shadow blocked the sun, her pulse kicked up a notch. She lowered her book, peeking over the top. In satisfying her curiosity she also sent her good mood into the basement. *Dammit.* Nobody was that unlucky. First, he'd dogged her every move yesterday, and now it seemed as if Connor St. James was destined to plague her vacation. Despite his suggestion they let the past stay where it was, she had her doubts she could do that. Even if his kiss was enough to curl her toes, twenty years of history were hard to overcome.

Connor flung himself lazily into the chair Stephanie vacated moments before. "You'll burn," he said, his gaze raking over her bikini-clad body.

Avery covered her bare midriff with her book, resolving to make this short and sweet. "Sunscreen," she offered and then raised the book hoping he took the hint.

"It's important to reapply." He reached for the bottle of sunscreen sitting on the little table she'd brought down from the pool area. "I'd be only too happy to help with that."

She drew her legs into her body. "I've got that covered." She'd stay inside her hotel room or suffer second-degree burns before she'd ask him for help. Although…the mental image of his hands on her chased

31

away the goose bumps. "What are you doing here?" she asked, tamping down the mental image.

"Not stalking you, if you were wondering." Connor jutted his chin toward the cove behind them. "I keep my boat docked here at the marina. I'm doing some repairs for a few days."

Of course he was. She groaned inwardly. *God, that was Connor who she'd lusted after this morning.* Avery cut her eyes at him. She didn't remember him being quite that buff when they'd both been part of Admiral Griffin's squadron. He'd always been a handsome devil; she'd never denied that. Dressed in a tight T-shirt and long shorts, he looked even better than he had as a younger man.

"So the question is, what are you doing on my beach?"

It seemed as if he derived some demented pleasure at riling her so maybe if she was polite he'd go away quicker. "I'm on vacation. This part of the coast is beautiful," she said, offering him a pleasant smile.

"Lots of beautiful things on the beach this morning."

The corners of his eyes crinkled as he smiled, and she couldn't help fixating on the blue that matched the water behind her. Avery almost wished he were sniping at her rather than looking at her with that earnest expression. This wasn't the way their relationship worked. If they spoke at all it was a dig at the other's flying prowess or some similar barbed comment. Even last night he'd started their conversation by accusing her of getting ready to drive drunk. The heated looks and subtle suggestions didn't fit. "I didn't know you were into boats," she said.

His gaze never left hers. "There's a lot about me you don't know," he countered then edged his chair closer to hers.

"I know enough." She looked away.

The difference between them was more than professional rivalry. She lived by the numbers, following the navy's flight guidelines to the letter. Whereas, he liked to skirt the edges, especially if it gained him the upper hand.

"Besides the fact that I'm a better pilot than you, what do you know about me?"

He also had a healthy opinion of himself. *Don't take the bait.* But dammit, she couldn't let this go. Connor's skills behind the stick might be legendary, but she'd pit her abilities against his any day. And she'd do it following the rules.

"I know you like to steal things." She bit the words out. She'd been top of their training class at NAS Whiting Field with him coming in a close second. On their last exercise before graduation, he'd beaten her out of the top spot by flying outside the box. The fact he'd gotten away with the stunt still rankled years later, especially since it garnered him the appointment that should have been hers.

Heat flashed in his blue eyes. "What have I ever stolen from you other than that kiss last night?"

Without meaning to, her mind raced back to her childhood. "You stole my first kiss as well."

"That's all right." Connor shrugged. "You've done worse." He fixed her with a stare. "And I'm not talking about when you promptly punched me in the nose after I kissed you outside Miss Hendricks's algebra class."

Avery blinked, surprised he remembered that much

detail about their kiss. But what was he alluding to? She couldn't remember a time when she exacted any type of retribution. Despite knowing better, curiosity piqued her interest. "When exactly did this payback occur?"

"You took my virginity."

Her mouth opened. "I did not," she finally managed after a moment. Their one-time only event came rushing back with twenty-twenty clarity. Her body heated as she remembered. It sure seemed like he'd known what to do. "Surely it wasn't." For a pair of fumbling eighteen-year-olds, it had been a tender lovemaking that colored her expectations for the rest of her life.

After an absence in each other's lives for six years, they'd reconnected as plebes at the Academy. They'd actually gotten along, and Avery considered Connor a friend of sorts. He'd treated her fairly back then, neither condescendingly as some of the other male cadets had nor with animosity. When she'd gotten a Dear Jane letter, she'd snuck out of her dorm to talk things over with Connor. With a couple illicit beers under their belts…

"You did, and it was." Connor leaned close enough for her to catch a whiff of his cologne. Warm and spicy, it added to her already befuddled condition.

Avery's cheeks heated. It hadn't been her first time. Her high school boyfriend had that honor. "But you were…" *magnificent, tender, knowing.*

Again her words died before they reached her tongue. She remembered that night like it had happened this morning instead of years ago. Better than her first time with what's-his-name, or the last time with Rob on the night she'd come home from deployment. *God, what a humiliation that had been.*

Connor had been so confident as he'd stripped her out of her clothes and then made love to her on his bunk. Avery checked his expression, searching for some sign he was once again yanking her chain.

Nothing but sincerity shone back in his blue eyes.

"I didn't know," she said. It did help fill in the holes about the aftermath of them making love. "I'm sorry…" The years-too-late apology dried up. The next day, he'd found her between classes. When he tried to talk about what happened, she'd brushed his affectionate advances away. There was no defense for how she'd handled things, other than to say she'd woken up the next morning with a killer hangover and the certain knowledge that falling in love with another plebe would sidetrack both their careers. "I really am sorry," she said, meaning it to her soul.

"No worries." The corner of his mouth turned up. "So we're even then?" he asked.

She fought the smile playing at her lips. If he could let go the way she trampled his ego, who was she to hold onto a professional rivalry? "Yeah, I guess we are."

He nodded as if they'd settled the matter. "Friends then?"

Avery looked at the rugged hand he offered, wondering what it would feel like against her skin. "Okay." She extended her hand and found out. The warmth sent small tremors through her body, building pockets of desire in places she hadn't felt physical need in years. Her breath caught.

Connor tugged on the hand he held in his, focusing her attention on him, then with his other he fingered one of her curls that had come loose from her ponytail. "How is it possible you've gotten more beautiful?"

Pulling out of a 5G dive was easier than pulling out of his grasp, especially with the urge to sink into his arms so strong. Avery dug deep and snatched her hand from his. "I don't think this is a good idea," she said, though at the moment she'd have trouble saying specifically what was wrong with letting him continue to brush his thumb across her cheek.

Connor shrugged. "Maybe not. But it doesn't mean we won't have fun doing it."

Being with him would be like putting her plane in a dive—exhilarating as hell and just as dangerous. She should send him on his merry way with a couple well-placed sharp words.

His offer dangled tantalizingly in the air between them.

She wanted Connor. There was no sense in lying to herself about that. She also wanted a twenty-pound box of chocolate. In the long run, neither would be good for her.

The alarm on her phone sounded, saving her from making a huge mistake. "I've got an appointment I need to keep," she said, snatching her things and practically sprinting to her hotel room.

Chapter Four

Moments later Avery punched in her ex's cell phone number on her tablet. While she waited for the call to go through, she tapped her toe against the balcony railing. From her room on the fifth floor, she could clearly see Titan's boat bobbing in the marina. Despite the questions swirling around in her head, she'd have to wait to give her encounter with him the airtime it needed.

The tradition of video conferencing with Will dated to her first deployment after his birth. Back then Rob held their six-month-old up to the screen. The pain of separation from her baby still echoed in her chest. Thank God this separation was short, and she had her own vacation to distract her.

After a brief word with Rob, her son's face filled the screen. "Hey, buddy." His cheeks had a kiss of sun on them, and she dreaded when they'd lose their fullness. "How's Florida?"

He offered her a snaggletooth grin. "It's awesome. Dad and I went body surfing yesterday, and Tiffany bought me a new game for my gaming system."

Avery stiffened at the mention of Rob's current girlfriend, and Hank's former wife. She plastered a smile on her face. "That's wonderful. Sounds like you three are having a great vacation."

At least Rob had settled down with one of the

women he'd been screwing. "What's your plan for the next few days?"

"Dad and Tiff…" His smile faltered, sending her pulse into triple digits.

"What's going on?" she asked. If Rob was ignoring Will in favor of Miss Thang, it would be the last time she let her ex take him for a whole week.

"Well." He nibbled his thumb, a habit he'd gotten from her.

Avery bit back the urge to hurry him along. Instead, she waited while her mind ran through all kinds of worst-case scenarios. God, she hoped Rob hadn't promised to buy him a Seadoo or to take him parasailing. Rob was long on extravagant presents and short on common sense.

"Dad and Tiff are getting married on the beach tomorrow. Granny, Pop, and Tiffany's family just got here a little while ago," Will said in a rush of words.

It was a second before she could reply. Though she and Rob had been divorced over a year, the sting of regret and failure often seemed as fresh as when she'd first served him with papers. He'd been the first to leave the marriage, his infidelity being the beginning salvo. Now he was the first to officially move on. She squashed the myriad of emotions bubbling up. This wasn't about her. His feelings about gaining a stepmom trumped hers of regret.

"Wow," Avery began, keeping her voice light. "That's a surprise. Did you know that before you left Atlanta?"

Will shook his head. "No, Dad told me on the way down." Then he pulled his thumb away from his mouth and met her gaze. "He said I get to hold the rings."

She forced a smile to her lips. "That's awesome, buddy. I know you'll do a great job."

All the tension melted from Will's face, replaced with a smile. "I know. I'm excited. He said I get to wear a suit just like him and Uncle Mac."

"I'm so proud of you." She might never make captain or shatter the glass ceiling at Flight Innovations, but she'd managed to raise a fantastic son.

Rob's voice called from the background, and Will turned from the screen to answer. "Just a minute, Dad, I'm talking with Mom."

"You go on," she told him. "Have a good time, and you can tell me all about the wedding when we talk tomorrow."

Will didn't immediately end the call. Instead his brown eyes connected to hers. "Love you, Mom." His anxiety showed clearly through the screen. He was worried about her.

She widened her eyes to keep the tears from spilling. Not because her ex-husband moved on first, but because she was blessed with such a sweet, sensitive son, who didn't need to be worried about her feelings.

"Love you, too, buddy," she said, her voice coming out thin and reedy.

Only after Avery hit the End button did she give into her emotions. She thumbed away her tears then gathered her notebook. Worrying over a son who was obviously having a great time or throwing herself a pity party wasn't accomplishing a damned thing.

Something wasn't right though, and it wasn't just the fact her ex-husband was marrying a woman who had the morals of a tomcat. They were two peas in a pod as far as she was concerned. She tugged on the sliding glass door, stepping inside her room. Why hadn't Rob told Will about the wedding sooner than a day before? It could be Rob had gotten himself into a baby momma situation and suddenly decided to make an honest woman out of Tiffany.

No, that wasn't it. Anxiety morphed into a full-blown sense of foreboding. She'd learned long ago to listen to that still, small voice when it started sending up warning flares. She'd ignored the warning signs before, and she swore she'd never let any man play her for a fool again. As much as she wanted to dig until she uncovered what her well-developed bullshit meter was telling her, she'd have to wait till Saturday to find out what Rob had up his sleeve.

After her video conference with Will, she spent the next hour trying catch up on her backlog of work. Only any type of concentration wasn't happening, not after the little news bomb that had been dropped in her lap. Finally, she gave up and headed back down to the beach to catch up with the Collins family.

Stephanie looked up from the magazine she was reading. "You know what they say. All work and no play…" she said as Avery plopped down in the chaise lounge next to her.

She tried not to think about the fifty emails sitting in her Inbox. Or the voice of anxiety that wouldn't be quiet. "I wasn't just working. Will and I had our daily video visit."

"Is he having a good time with his dad?" Stephanie asked.

As much as Avery wanted to hash out her worries, she didn't want to put a damper on everyone's vacation mood. "He's fine," she said, reaching for her book.

Minutes later Opie hauled himself out of the pool where he'd been playing with his kids. After a quick kiss to his wife's cheek, he plopped into the lounge chair next to her. "Everything okay with Will?"

After years of working together, she knew better than to try and lie to her wingman. It also didn't help her attempt at deflection that she was, like Will had been earlier, chewing on her thumb. She tucked her hand under her thigh. "Sure," she said, still trying to get her head around the news.

Opie leaned forward, making eye contact with her. "Do you and I need to go get the boy? I can have us on I-95 south in about an hour."

Avery gripped the arm of her chaise lounge, suppressing the sudden urge to hug him. "No. He's fine. Will had some unexpected news, that's all."

Stephanie put down the magazine she'd been reading. "Spill it," she ordered, turning her attention to Avery.

"So it looks like Rob and Hank's ex are getting hitched."

Minutes later Stephanie's eyes were still wide as she finished recapping her video conference with Will. "They deserve each other."

"As long as Miss Thang doesn't keep Will from spending time with his dad, I'm all right with Rob remarrying." Avery rolled her eyes. "It's not like I want him."

Stephanie patted her on the knee. "You know what they say: living well is its own revenge."

"I guess it is," Avery said. To a degree she'd put her divorce in her rearview mirror. Atlanta was

41

beginning to feel like home. She planned to use the bonus she would earn from winning the Carolina Entertainment account to put a down payment on a house. She'd even gone on a couple dates. They hadn't gone well. Despite enjoying getting dolled up with cute shoes and a good mani/pedi, she wasn't soft and sweet like most men wanted. She called things like she saw them, and that put off a lot of guys.

Her gaze gravitated to Connor's boat, hoping to catch a glimpse of him working topside. With a view of the stern, she could read the name of his boat. *The Nemesis.* She smiled. Before their meeting on the beach, that would have clearly defined their relationship. Between his revelation that she'd been his first lover and his suggestion she be his next, she couldn't cling to their rivalry any longer. But did she want to take things to a different level with him?

Stephanie waved a hand in front of Avery's face, pulling her out of her musings. "You're not hearing a word I've said."

"I'm sorry. What's that?

"It's time for our massage."

"Excellent," she said, grabbing her towel. She cast one last look over her shoulder as she stepped inside the hotel. Maybe later on she'd walk down to the docks to see if he was interested in having lunch. Yeah, sharing meal together would probably be a safe way to explore her newly-formed friendship with him.

Jeez, her emotions were all over the place—discouraged about her ex moving on when she was still treading water, worried how Will would take the change. She glanced at Connor's boat again. Her body remembered the feel of his hand on her as he twirled a finger around her hair. Titan added another kink to her churning emotions. Lowering her sunglasses she squinted, trying to see if he'd returned from his errand.

****

Connor cut through the hotel's pool area instead of taking the winding path that led from the hotel's parking lot down to the marina. He told himself the choice was simply a matter of geometry. The shortest distance between two points was a straight line after all. Even he didn't believe the lie.

His personal life became nonexistent when he took on the responsibilities of Aviation Options and Sofia. His priority remained the care of his niece, but over the past few months he'd yearned to recapture some of the life he'd led. What had been restlessness exploded into a burning need when he kissed Avery last night.

He scanned the pool area, anticipation kicking his pulse up a couple notches. There were a number of mostly unclothed beauties edging the pool area. None of them came close to her appeal. God, she'd been gorgeous in her tiny blue bikini. Her sweet apology rang in his ears. Hell, he'd been an eager participant in his first sexual experience, but it was nice to know she'd wished things had been different afterward.

A flash of blue caught his attention, and he turned in time to see Avery and Stephanie stepping inside the hotel. He had a dozen things to keep him busy. None would likely give him the charge a simple conversation with her would. Or the raw lust she evoked.

Following his gut instead of his brain, Connor headed to the line of lounge chairs that ringed the pool. "I see the ladies have abandoned you," he said to Opie.

The guy motioned to the hotel. "Yeah, they went in

for massages."

A vision of her creamy skin bloomed in his imagination. "Sounds like a good way to spend an hour."

Maybe if he scratched this itch, he'd be able to let go of the Avery fantasies that kept him awake last night. Hell, who was he kidding? She'd been plaguing him in one way or another for most of his life.

Now that he thought back with a little more clarity than he'd possessed at age eighteen, he saw the wisdom of her decision at the time. Nothing was stopping them now, though, except that she acted more likely to take a swing at him than to fall passionately into his arms. At least he'd get a reaction, one way or the other. If he let this opportunity pass, he'd always wonder what might have happened. What did he have to lose?

"I'll catch you later," Connor said.

"Sure," Opie said, eyeing him

Connor made a beeline for his boat, stowing the supplies and parts he'd bought in town. If things went the way he hoped, he'd get back to them at a much later time. Returning to the hotel, he followed the signage to the spa area. Ahead, he saw a young woman dressed in the hotel's signature blue and yellow uniform.

He caught up to her as she put her hand to the door knob. "Excuse me," he said, noting the bottle of massage oil in her hand. "I was hoping you'd help me surprise my girlfriend. Is this Avery Madigan's room?"

Ninety seconds and fifty bucks later Connor's do-or-die plan was wheels up and feet wet. Either this would work, and the two of them could finally explore the attraction they'd been denying for so many years, or he'd go down in flames.

Chapter Five

A tinkling chime played in the background as Avery lay face down on the massage table. She let out a breath, determined to put a stop to her jumbled thoughts. Warm sheets covered her, giving a lovely feeling of protection. While her body could be fooled into relaxing, her mind wasn't so easy to get on board.

Learning Rob was remarrying shouldn't have bothered her so much. The wounds of his infidelity had healed into scars and what she'd told Stephanie was the truth. She didn't want Rob back. But she didn't want him to be the first to move on either. Seemed like karma should have dictated the one who'd been faithful to the marriage should reap the rewards. *I guess it doesn't work quite like that.*

Snuggling into the warm blankets, Avery renewed her determination to move on with her life. *Alpha, bravo, charlie...* She recited the military alphabet in an attempt to clear her mind.

Her mind involuntarily shot to Connor. Despite their history and his annoying persistence, he was growing on her. Maybe he'd changed in the past few years. She sure had. At the soft snick of the door opening and closing again, she let out a slow breath. *Delta, echo, foxtrot.* She needed this massage if the people in her world continued turning it on its ear.

The masseuse drew the sheet off her shoulders and

began kneading Avery's trap muscles. The firm stokes didn't match with the petite woman she'd met minutes before, but they sure were working magic on her tension.

Something wasn't quite right.

Maybe it was her well-developed sixth sense, or the way the masseuse's calloused fingers abraded the knot in her neck, but something didn't jive. She cracked an eyelid, spying a pair of sandaled feet that clearly belonged to a man.

"What the…" She performed the tricky maneuver of snatching the sheet to cover her nakedness while sitting up.

Connor shot her a grin. "Hi."

Avery clutched the sheet tighter. "What do you think you're doing?"

"Helping you relax," he said, trailing a finger up her arm.

She jerked away. "You are not."

"You liked it." His hand continued its path up her arm sending licks of desire along with it. "I could tell."

So, who wouldn't have? The guy had good hands. "You have a monstrous ego, you know that, right?"

He shrugged. "I don't see what the problem is."

She rolled her eyes. Wasn't that the God's honest truth. "See." She stabbed a finger into his hard chest. "This is why we can't get along. You don't play by the rules."

"What rules am I breaking?" Fire danced in his blue eyes.

Her brain went offline. "I can't think of any right now." Even if he hadn't broken any rules per se, he was definitely invading her privacy. And getting her hot.

"You shouldn't have come here."

"I wanted to help you relax." He spoke in soothing tones as if he were trying to calm a frightened animal. His strong fingers dug into her shoulders. She should have moved away from him, but she couldn't muster the will. He was right. Her body seemed to yield to his ministrations. "Your shoulders are up around your ears. Do you ever relax?"

His query snapped her out of this thrall. Far from relaxing, he was heating her body to the boiling point. "That's what I was supposed to be doing."

His fingers found a particularly tender spot on her neck. "Oh, God." She groaned without meaning to. "Right there." Jeez, he'd missed his calling.

"Like this?" he asked, working the knot from her neck.

She made an agreeable noise. With his hands continuing their magic, her anger melted along with her tension. Somewhere in the back of her mind floated all the reasons agreeing to his plan would end badly. For the moment, she couldn't muster the will to act on them.

"Lie back down," he told her.

Avery's gaze shot to his. What was he planning to do?

****

Connor sensed the unspoken question in her gaze. "Nothing's going to happen that you don't want, sweetheart." His words were both a promise that she could bring things to a stop if she wanted and a statement of fact. He knew she wanted him, could see it in her eyes and the way she responded to his touch.

"Go ahead," he urged.

47

Male pride roared with satisfaction when she complied with his demand by rolling onto her stomach. He slid the sheet down several inches to discover a beautifully done tattoo graced her back. The curlicues traced the flare of her hip then dipped below the sheet. As much as his curiosity begged to discover how much skin the tattoo covered, he resisted the urge. Instead, he stayed to the gentle dips and valleys of her back.

Inch by inch was the way to win this particular scrimmage, and he was damned determined to win her over. When he'd worked her back and arms, he re-covered them. "I'm doing your legs now," he said, playing the part of masseuse to the hilt.

The single nod she gave shouldn't have pleased him so much. But it did. It also made him want to do more things to bring her pleasure. Connor poured more oil into his hands and moved to the end of the table. He dug his fingers into the arch of her foot, eliciting a low groan.

He couldn't help the chuckle. "I told you so."

Over the next few minutes he worked his way to her knees. By then her breaths came in long intervals. If he were any type of gentleman, he would have quietly slipped out of the room at this point. He'd helped her relax as he'd offered to do. Connor gave that option barely a passing thought. Instead, he placed a palm on the back of Avery's thigh, signaling his intentions.

Her body tensed but for a second before she nodded her consent. Connor slid his hand beneath the sheet. As much as his eyes craved the sight of her bare ass, this wasn't the moment for his own gratification. This was all about her.

Connor held his breath as he worked his way up

her thigh. How high up would she let him go? He'd never been the cautious type, and he wasn't about to start now. He delved further, letting his middle finger brush against her sex.

She rewarded him with a low groan that shot straight to his groin. Never had a woman been able to call his body to attention merely with the sound of her voice. Blood flooded his cock till it pressed painfully against his shorts. Ignoring its demand for attention, he stroked her delicate folds. Her essence coated his fingers, the erotic scent of her arousal filling his nostrils. He licked his lips, wanting to add taste to the senses fully involved in bringing Avery pleasure.

Using the evidence of her arousal he eased the friction, teasing the bundle of nerves at the top of her sex. Her hips moved in concert with his hands, growing more urgent and mesmerizing as he watched her chase an orgasm. He pressed his thumb inside her core, stroking her with one hand while he kneaded her ass with the other. Her pleasure crested, and she came with a low moan that echoed around the room. Finally, the tremors gentled and she grew still.

"Oh, God," she groaned, pushing against his hands. Avery curled up and hid her face behind her hands.

"Don't," he said, tugging them away. He leaned in to whisper. "You were beautiful."

She raised her head from the massage table, her gaze meeting his. Heat infused her gray eyes. "I can't believe I let you do that to me."

Connor couldn't either. "I realized something today," he said, leaning close. "We've been dancing around our attraction our whole lives." He'd had many lovers over the years, had done far more adventurous

49

acts. None held the significance of bringing Avery to orgasm. He was dying to do it again. Only this time he wanted to be buried deep in her heat when she came. "I say it's time we gave in."

She sat up, drawing the sheet around her body. "I can't think."

Connor grasped her chin, tilting it to meet his gaze. "What is there to think about?"

Shaking her head, she lowered her eyes. This shy version of Avery was unlike the spit-and-vinegar version he'd known. Several tense heartbeats passed. Maybe he'd gone about this the wrong way, pushed her too hard. "I'll give you a couple minutes to dress, and then we'll have lunch."

She squared her shoulders. "I have a mani/pedi scheduled next."

He bit his lip to keep from laughing. There was the woman who'd challenged him at every turn. "Make it dinner, then. I'll meet you at the hotel's restaurant at seven tonight." He turned to go but stopped with his hand on the doorknob. From over his shoulder he told her, "We'll talk. But just so you know, we are going to happen."

****

Connor's parting words floated on the air. She envied his surety. Not so much that he thought they were certain to become lovers, but that he saw the inevitability as a good thing. He thought that because he didn't know something about her. Long after her ex-husband uttered bitter accusations, his voice still rattled around in her head. *You have no clue how to please a man.*

Avery sat on the massage table, the sheet still

wrapped around her naked body. Echoes of the orgasm Connor gave her still reverberated through her. He'd lulled her into accepting his ministrations, teasing her body to fevered need so that by the time his hand reached her sex she'd been dying for the release.

She could no more have stopped him than she could erase her history with him. Afterward as reality replaced the endorphins fogging her brain, she'd had the strength to put a stop to the speeding freight train. Not because she hadn't enjoyed what Connor was doing to her, but because she knew he'd want more. Hell, *she* wanted more. Visions of him taking her atop the massage table played through her brain.

Indulging in that would lead to disappointment on his part and further mortification on hers. She'd just have to explain things to him. Yeah, like how was that supposed to work*? I don't know what I'm doing.*

Avery climbed down from the table. After wrapping herself in a robe the spa gave her, she opened the door of the massage room to find Stephanie waiting for her.

"That must have been some massage. You look limp as a dishrag."

Heat crept to her cheeks. "It was pretty good." That was the understatement of the century.

Minutes later they were seated in a comfy chair, a pair of nail technicians busy working them over. "David and the kids want seafood tonight. I thought we'd drive up the coast for dinner," Stephanie said through the towel the cosmetologist had wrapped around her face.

Avery shot a glance toward her friend. She wouldn't lie, but she wasn't exactly ready to share her plans either. Better to keep the awkward moments to a minimum. "Would you mind if I took a rain check?"

"What? You don't want to eat at Captain Billy's?" she asked, mentioning a locally famous restaurant that boasted a fifty-foot all-you-can-eat buffet.

"I have some things I need to take care of tonight. Tell Opie he can eat my share of boiled shrimp."

"I don't blame you. I'd take a pass, too, if I could get away with it," Stephanie said, then leaned back in her chair.

When Avery and Stephanie were sugar-scrubbed, waxed, and polished within an inch of their lives, they left the spa area of the hotel. Walking through the lobby, Avery glanced toward the restaurant. She had an hour before she was supposed to meet Connor. Her stomach knotted thinking about the conversation she needed to have with him.

She took the elevator with Stephanie to their hotel rooms on the fifth floor.

"Poolside breakfast?" Stephanie asked, pausing at her door.

Avery slid her keycard in the door of her room. She'd probably need a pitcher of mimosas after she got through explaining things to Connor. "Sure. Nine o'clock good for you?"

"Don't work too much," Stephanie said before slipping inside her room.

Once inside her hotel room, Avery padded to the closet where she'd hung her dress whites and the suit she'd wear to her meeting on Friday. She'd also packed a couple sundresses, knowing they planned to eat dinner out most nights. Avery fingered the coral and turquoise dress before slipping it off the hanger.

Her dinner with Connor wasn't a date, even though she wanted it to be. She'd seen sides of him she liked—much to her surprise. Too bad she hadn't seen his attributes years ago. She put the dress on anyway. Maybe if she felt pretty, it would bolster her courage to tell Connor the truth. As much as she might want the two of them to explore their attraction, she couldn't. Avery had experienced all the humiliation at the hands of a lover that her wounded soul could take. It was better to turn him down now and hope it didn't ruin their newfound friendship than for him to learn the truth. She was as hopeless at reciprocating the passion he'd shown her as she was at cooking. She grabbed her purse, stuffing her cell phone and the keycard inside. She was several minutes early, but she'd lose her nerve if she waited.

Downstairs in the hotel's restaurant, she paced in front of the hostess' podium. *While I enjoyed what happened earlier*—no, that sounded as if they'd had pizza and a movie. Besides, enjoyment didn't begin to adequately describe what he'd given her. God, if that's what he could do during foreplay…she couldn't imagine how good actual penetration would be.

It also didn't address what Connor had been really suggesting, that they become lovers. *Now that we're friends, I'd like to keep it that way.* At least she hoped after she turned him down he'd still be willing to lay their previous animosity aside.

Despite the distraction Connor provided, her sixth sense kept bringing her back around to the situation with Rob. She hadn't spent four years married to the guy and not learned when he was up to something. If she had to go twenty rounds with him over child

53

support or visitation, she needed a few more people in her corner. At least she believed she could trust Connor. After all, with them both working civilian jobs, the only thing they'd have to compete over was if the two of them played pool. She didn't think he had that in mind as he stepped in view.

After striding across the hotel lobby like he owned the place, Connor brushed a kiss against her cheek. "You're early," he said, the whiskers of his goatee tickling her cheek. "Were you anxious to see me again?"

She'd always admired his confidence, even when it was backed up with nothing more than BS. "Maybe." She fought to keep the smile from her lips. He was already charming his way past her defenses, and they were still standing at the front of the restaurant.

Avery slipped from his grasp as the hostess returned to her station. If she had any chance of carrying on a rational conversation, she had to keep her wits about her. And Connor had a way of clouding her judgment better than any man or amount of alcohol ever could.

"Reservation for two under the name of St. James," he told the hostess.

The college-aged woman snapped up two leather bound menus and motioned toward the interior of the restaurant. "We have the table you requested ready for you, sir."

Dressed in a dark suit and tie, he seemed more like a business mogul than the jet jockey he'd once been. He certainly carried himself as one who was accustomed to having his orders obeyed. She combed the recesses of her memory trying to recall exactly what enterprise had backed his family's admission into LaGrange's upper echelons.

They followed the hostess to a booth in a quiet corner of the restaurant. Instead of taking the bench across from her, Connor slid in next to her. She eyed him questioningly. He wouldn't make turning him down easy, especially as he put his arm around her bare shoulders.

"I was afraid you'd change your mind," he murmured, fingering her hair. "I had a feeling you'd start overthinking what happened."

Her heart thudded in her chest. Between the feel of his body next to hers and his heated gaze, her brain would turn to mush before she got out what she had to say. "I haven't changed my mind about dinner," she said, creating a little space between their bodies. "We have a lot of catching up to do."

Connor cupped her cheek, his thumb tracing across her bottom lip. "I wasn't talking about having a meal with me. I have a sneaking suspicion you spent your spa time thinking of all the reasons why we shouldn't give a little air time to our attraction."

She picked up the menu so he couldn't see how true his suspicions were. "What looks good?" she asked.

Connor chuckled as he mirrored her own actions. "The seafood here is good, but I think I need a nice juicy steak." He cut his gaze to her. "I need to keep up my strength."

Avery snapped the menu closed, deciding to get the awkward conversation she needed to have with Connor out of the way. "I need to…"

Before she could get any further, his phone began

vibrating in his pocket.

He shot her an apologetic look as he reached for it. "I've got a couple situations brewing back home, so I've got to take this." Looking at the screen, he let out a breath. "What's up, Sofia?" he asked.

As he listened, he began running his hand through his hair. "Who else is going?" he asked. Several more seconds of silence on his part ticked past. "Curfew is still eleven, and I want you to call me when you get back to the Barnes' home. Have fun and be good," he said before ending the call.

How had she not known he had a child? A teenaged daughter from the sounds of the conversation.

"My niece, Sofia," he said, in answer to her unspoken question. "She came to live with me three years ago after my brother died."

It seemed that both their lives had come unraveled at the same time. "I'm sorry for your loss and hers," she said, squeezing his hand.

A dark shadow passed over his face, making Avery think there was more to the story than he was sharing. "Thank you. The past couple years have been hard for her," he said, then picked up the wine menu. "Can I tempt you with a drink? Since neither of us has to drive, I say we treat ourselves tonight."

She swallowed hard. "Let's hold off for a moment. First, I have a few things you need to know about me."

His gaze danced over her. "I know you want me. What else is there to know?"

As much as her body yearned for him, her mind and heart couldn't get on board with that plan. "I don't do one-night stands," she said. Maybe if they had weeks or months together, he could teach her how to please him.

Heat infused his gaze. "Who says this one night would be enough."

Her pulse thrummed in her ears. It wouldn't be, and that was part of the problem. "I have to leave Friday after a meeting."

Connor brushed back her hair. "That gives us a couple days," he drawled. "Do you do two-night stands?"

Avery pushed against his chest to keep him from leaning in further. The heat radiating off his body mixed with his spicy masculine scent and clouded her thoughts. "Oh, this is such a bad idea." She groaned. Even if her lack of sexual prowess wasn't a factor, there was the little matter of her heart. Sure, she'd been all for the idea—in theory. In practice—Connor was the wrong guy for a dozen different reasons. But she wanted another taste of what he'd given her earlier.

"You're thinking about it, though, aren't you?"

She nodded. Hell, it was all she could think about.

"I swear I'll make this the best vacation you've ever had," he said.

She wasn't willing to slam the door shut on the possibility. But she wasn't prepared to blow the doors off either. "Two days and at the end we walk away, none the worse for the experience."

Connor arched an eyebrow. "I'd like to think we'll be all the better."

Avery fumbled with her napkin. "So how does this work? Do we just race to the elevator ripping off each other's clothes?"

"I like the way your mind works," he said, shooting her a devilish grin. "But, I did promise you dinner."

Chapter Six

Connor brushed back a lock of Avery's hair to improve the already gorgeous view. The glass of red wine had put a lovely blush on her cheeks and gotten her to loosen up a bit. The corner of her eyes crinkled with amusement. "So I told the guy, if I tell you, I'll have to kill you.'" Her plump lips curled in a smile. "Needless to say, I didn't get that job." Her laughter dried up as she glanced over and caught him staring.

He looked away. "Good to hear I'm not the only one making a less than perfect transition into civilian work," he said, covering for the fact he'd been only half listening to her story about her first post-navy interview. Kinda hard to concentrate on small talk when the graceful curves of her neck and shoulders absorbed all his attention.

"Well, it wasn't exactly the most intelligent answer I've ever given, but I was nervous and the guy was being a jerk."

The two of them managed to get through the three-course meal with just a handful of awkward moments like this one, times where one of them remembered what would happen at the end of the meal.

Connor could think of little else. The steak he ordered tasted like the bottom of his shoe, though that was probably not any fault of the chef. With Avery's body next to his, he was jonesing to get her somewhere private. His hand brushed along the hem of her skirt, feeling the silkiness of her stockings.

She stopped him from sliding his hand further up her leg. "Jeez, Titan, people will see."

He nodded and began fondling the stem of his wine glass instead. After the bus boy cleared their dishes, the waiter approached the table for what seemed like the hundredth time. For once Connor would have loved to have a lazy waiter.

"Could I interest either of you in dessert?" the college-aged guy asked.

"No, thank you," Connor said. He shot Avery a look, one he hoped would let her know what—or rather who—he wanted as an after-dinner treat.

Her cheeks pinked; something he never imagined he'd see on her. Perhaps she, too, was recalling what he'd done to her earlier in the day.

After bringing Avery to orgasm in the massage room, the scent of her arousal had coated his fingers and filled his head for hours afterward. Even as he sat there, he imagined he caught a wisp of her natural scent.

"What if I wanted dessert?" she asked once the waiter left. Her mouth turned up as she shot him a look from the corner of her eye. "Something else you don't know about me, I have a huge sweet tooth."

"Actually, I did know that." He brushed back her hair and leaned over to kiss the tender flesh where her neck met her shoulder. "I've already made arrangements for room service to deliver a tray to your room."

"Arrogant much?" She arched her eyebrows, but her accusation lacked heat. "Were you that certain I'd say 'yes'?"

Connor quickly paid the check and scooted them out of the booth. "It's not arrogance, baby, if you can back it up."

He steered Avery inside the elevator, her musical laugh ringing in his ears. "What would you have done if I'd turned you down?"

He stalked toward her as the doors closed them in. His arms bracketed her, hemming her in without actually touching her. "I knew you wouldn't," he murmured in her ear.

She drew in jagged breaths. "No, I probably wouldn't have."

When the elevator doors opened, she ducked underneath his arm and bolted for the corridor. Watching the subtle way her hips moved ahead of him had him rethinking his slow seduction tactic. Maybe next time, after he'd taken the edge off his hunger.

Avery opened the door to her room to reveal a small efficiency suite. She moved to the table and tossed her purse and key down next to an open laptop and a neat stack of papers. "Would you like coffee?"

His eyes shifted from watching her to the king-sized bed visible through a set of French doors. "Maybe later." He sat on the sofa in the living area of the suite and patted the cushion. "Come sit next to me."

"I sat next to you in the restaurant." She shook her head but moved toward him all the same.

When she sank to the sofa, he tugged her onto his lap. His desire for her barely controlled, he tilted her backward in his arms, putting her as off kilter as she'd made him. Connor wove his fingers through her hair, holding her head in place so he could plunder her mouth. She tasted of wine and a richness uniquely her own. "Yes," he said, pulling away to press kisses across her cheek. "But I had to behave myself in public."

His words came out like gravel. Even to his own ears they exposed just how close to the edge he was. Despite being a risk taker, his career as a pilot required him to be clear headed. Avery fogged his thinking to the point his only thoughts were of getting her naked and underneath him. He loved the feeling he was free falling even as it scared the shit out of him.

"That was behaving?" Her breasts pressed against his chest and her breath came in pants. "You had your hand halfway up my thigh."

Connor slid his hand again up her skirt to trace the lace holding her stockings in place. He loved the way the scent of her light perfume filled his nose and her silky skin set his alight. His barely controlled lust hung by the thinnest of wires. Everything Avery did stretched him to the breaking point.

A rap on the door stopped him from reminding her he'd never been the kind of guy who did anything halfway. Her eyes widened when the bellboy wheeled in the huge tray of desserts. "Maybe you know me better than I thought."

After signing the bill, he sent the bellboy on his way with a generous tip. With them alone again, he surveyed the tray of decadence—his plan for seduction. His gaze gravitated to the dish of strawberries. Choosing the choicest one, he dipped it in the bowl of warm chocolate, and then brought it to her lips. "Not as much as I'd like."

She bit into the berry, closing her eyes as she did. "God, that's good."

His cock hardened in answer to her moan. Connor repeated the process, feeding her one berry at a time. Did she have any idea what she was doing to him? If it had been any of the other women he'd bedded over the past few years, he would have said "yes." With her eyes closed and a little smile playing at her lips, he had to think not. Not that he'd mind her playing the vixen.

She reached for a napkin to dab away a trickle of juice. "Let me," he said, catching her hand.

Her eyes sprang open as his tongue darted out to capture the juice. He then covered her mouth with his. She opened readily when he licked at the seam of her lips. By the time she broke the kiss, they were both breathless. His hands moved along her arms and up to her sun-kissed shoulders. "Do you have any idea how many times I've remembered what you look like naked?"

He reached to her nape and unfastened the strap holding up her dress. As it fell to her waist, it revealed a pair of beautifully shaped beasts. Their peaks already formed tight buds just begging to be caressed.

Avery stood, taking his hand. "Let's go in the other room." Her suggestion proved he wasn't the only one affected by what they were doing to each other.

Connor scooped her up by way of an answer, carrying her into the next room. Then he kissed her down onto the bed. His tongue danced with hers, relishing the sweet taste of berry, chocolate, and her.

The tiny part of his brain not occupied with absorbing every sensation noted that although Avery's mouth moved against his and little moans of pleasure escaped her lips, her hands were nowhere near where they needed to be. A deep ache set up in his chest and radiated across his skin. "Touch me."

****

Avery fisted the sheets, wanting to do as Connor asked. To bring him the kind of incinerating pleasure he was so skillfully bringing her. Instead, her ex's words reverberated in her head and crowded out the pleasure of this moment. *Ice queen, ballbuster, rigid.*

During the last year of their marriage, Rob turned their attempts at lovemaking into critiques of everything he found lacking in her. She barely remembered herself as sexually confident. He found fault with everything. If she initiated sex, she was too aggressive. If she waited for him, she was too frigid. She wished to God she could get Rob's voice out of her head. And now she'd have to reveal her sexual ineptitude to Connor.

Before she could form the words, he spoke again. "I'm burning for your touch, Avery."

After a lifetime of keeping her weaknesses hidden and covering up her insecurities with sarcasm, she was ready for someone she could trust. Someone who wouldn't leverage her vulnerability for his own gain. "I'm not very good at this."

His gaze jerked to hers. "Who told you that? You've got me on the knife's edge, and you haven't even laid a hand on me."

That final confrontation she had with Rob flooded her mind. He said he needed a real woman to satisfy his needs, not some ballbuster. He even questioned her sexual orientation.

"That asshole," Connor growled as if he knew what happened. Or more likely, the shame showed on her face. She just didn't know how to please a man. Toward the end, she'd second-guessed every desire, every fantasy until it seemed better to lay back and let Rob use her body to get himself off.

"Did he blame you for his affairs?"

Avery couldn't escape the humiliation of having everyone in her squadron know what had happened. Within days of returning from deployment everyone from lowest seaman to Admiral Griffin knew of Rob's affairs. She forced the words past the lump in her throat. "I have a way of emasculating a man in case you haven't noticed."

Connor took her hand and placed it on his hard shaft. "Does that feel like emasculation?"

She stroked him, feeling his hard length in her palm. "No." She breathed the word.

"You've been making me hard for years."

"You don't feel threatened by me?" In his hungry gaze she began to reclaim the sexually confident woman she'd been not so many years before, especially as he barked out a laugh.

"Aggravated or challenged, but never emasculated."

Connor moved with infinite grace as he slid to the edge of the bed. Then he tugged her dress down her hips, revealing her nearly bare body one inch at a time. His gaze raked over her. "God, Avery, you're killing me here."

No matter how things ended when they parted after their agreed upon two days, she'd always be grateful to him for reminding her how much she enjoyed making love. How savoring another's body could be more than a biological imperative—that it could be fun.

"What?" Avery gave him her best innocent smile,

even batted her eyelashes a couple times. A sense of playfulness replaced the hesitance she'd felt moments before.

"That garter belt does sinful things to me. Did you put that on for me?"

"No. This is what I wear all the time." She ran her hand over the lace, and then reached to unclasp her stockings. "It makes me feel all girly."

"Girly, my ass," he said, gripping her hips. "That's a woman's body."

Electricity danced across her skin as he eased the stockings down her legs. She crooked her finger. "You want to know a secret?"

Connor nodded, his eyes taking on that devilish glint.

"I sometimes wore a thong and matching bra under uniform."

He groaned and collapsed onto the bed next to her.

"See, I don't always follow the rules," she said, turning on her side and caressing his well-muscled arm.

"I can see that." After unclasping her garter belt, Connor eased her onto her back. He traced the tattoo on her hip. "This isn't exactly navy issue either."

Avery thought about getting inked for years. While the navy restrictions only dealt with visible tattoos, it didn't prohibit those under her clothes. She'd chosen the vines and flowers that began at her right hip and curved around to end at the middle of her back. "I got it the day my divorce was final. I wanted something to prove to myself I was more than what people thought I was."

"You definitely are more than meets the eye," Connor said, biting his full lower lip. "Although what I

65

see is delicious, I can't wait to discover what else you've been hiding." Reaching down, he caught her by the back of her thighs, opening her up to him. "I have to taste you." He groaned as he slid his hand along her leg till he reached her sex. "I've been aching for you since we were in the massage room."

The stroke of his tongue against her secret flesh had her nearly bucking off the bed. With that single swipe, she became a wanton woman, desperate for pleasure. When she would have worked her cleft over his willing mouth, he gently held her still, pressing his palms to her inner thighs and opening her wider for his artful tongue-lashing. With every stroke, the tension in her core wound tighter and her need for release grew more urgent. Being her lifelong torturer, he didn't see fit to bring her to an immediate climax. Instead, just as an orgasm was within reach, he turned his attention to her core. After several such tortuous circuits, she growled out her frustration.

He chuckled darkly against her mound, but never altered the tactic that slowly drove her toward madness one swipe of the tongue at a time. When she could stand no more, she grabbed a hank of his hair anchoring his mouth to the spot where she needed it. Connor answered her unspoken plea for mercy by inserting two fingers into her channel and stroking a certain delicious spot. With a gasp she flew apart, riding the crest of ecstasy until it slowed to gentle waves.

While she was still a quaking mess, he pressed a single kiss to her cleft then crawled the length of her body. "You taste mighty fine, Mad," he said. Then he pressed his lips to hers, reigniting her need.

"Take me, Connor. I need you inside me."

His grin widened. "Oh, that's exactly where I'm headed." He reached to the floor for his trousers then, after extracting a foil packet from his pocket, quickly rolled on the condom. Arching over her, his erection nudged her. "Open for me, babe. Let me love you."

Her heart jolted at his words. But even as she reminded herself they were simply that—words spoken in a moment of passion—she tilted her hips and took him into her body. The slide of his erection along her core had her groaning. He thrust and retreated with excruciatingly slow strokes that made her greedy. "More," she pleaded, hooking her ankles over his ass. She raked her nails over his back wanting him deeper so that days later she'd still feel the echoes of his presence.

"That's it," he urged, his voice so low and gravely it sent shock waves through her chest. His hooded gaze latched on to hers. "Make me yours."

She wanted him to be hers, and for the few moments their bodies were joined, she'd let herself believe he was. He trailed hot kisses across her cheek then took her earlobe between his teeth giving it a nip that nearly sent her over the edge. She turned her cheek, offering him access to the sensitive flesh of her neck. Once again he answered her unspoken request, nibbling his way down to her collarbone as he stroked the flames of their passion higher. When he reached her breast, he suckled with deep draws that echoed in her core.

Finally, his slow, easy rhythm took on an urgent quality that matched the tension growing inside her. His breaths came in pants. "You're so wet. I don't know how long I can hold out." He adjusted the angle of his hips, rubbing against her clit with his thrust.

A moan escaped her lips that sounded nothing like her voice. More animal than woman, she was truly nothing like the person she projected to the world. He did this to her, brought out aspects of herself she'd kept buried beneath layers of armor. She kicked back her head and let her inner harlot take over.

"That's it, baby," he said, stroking her harder, faster. "Give it up to me."

At his command, she orgasmed hard. She cried out her pleasure until she was breathless and her vision faded. He followed soon after, finding his release with a roar that lay to rest any lingering doubt she might have had about her sexual prowess. Then he collapsed against her, breathing heavily. "I think I might have died a little bit back there," he said chuckling.

"We can't have that," she said, burying her face in the crook of his neck. She was still smiling when he planted a quick kiss to her cheek.

"I'll be right back."

When he pulled out of her, she immediately felt the loss. Avery clenched her eyelids against the onslaught of raw emotion. *Two days, one of which was nearly gone.* He returned with a washcloth while she was still reminding herself this was nothing more than a vacation fling.

"Gotta take care of you," he said, cleaning her with tenderness that touched her more than she was willing to admit.

"I'm good," she said, pushing his hand aside when the intimacy grew too much for her to handle. His brow furrowed, but he didn't comment. Instead, he dropped the cloth to the floor and crawled in beside her. As if they'd done this a thousand times before, he drew her in tight and turned them on their sides so their bodies fused from shoulder to hips. Then he threw a heavy leg over her hip, cupped her breast in his palm and buried his nose in her hair. Soon, slow breaths tickled her ear.

She gave over to the feeling of sated bliss, and nestled more firmly into the cradle of his hips. His strong arms made her feel cosseted rather than trapped. In those moments of passion something happened between them that went further than the act of sex. A transference of something—but of what? Twisting in his embrace, she brushed her hand through his hair as he dozed. What was she getting, more than the best sex of her life? More importantly, what was she giving away? Avery drew in a breath. As her pulse continued to pound, she had a feeling it was that part of her still beating at ninety miles an hour.

Chapter Seven

Hours after switching off the light, Connor woke with a start, his heart pounding, lungs working to draw in breath. Further down his cock pounded, an orgasm poised for release. He'd been dreaming of making love to Avery on the deck of his boat. They were far out to sea, and the waves offered just enough pitch to add a little piston action to their thrusts. With the sun beating down on his bare back, it was one of the most erotic dreams his imagination had ever conjured up.

Still asleep she rolled over, throwing her leg across his hips. Her hand trailed across his stomach as she nuzzled into his neck. He had a damned good imagination, but it was nothing compared to the real thing. Especially when she rubbed against him like a cat. He groaned with need, despite his having made love to her twice in as many hours.

"I must not have done something right if you're still awake," she murmured in the dark.

"That's not it," he said, kissing hair that smelled of coconut shampoo. Lying next to her had never seemed more right. He'd never be satisfied with just the couple days they'd agreed upon. "I have a lot of things on my mind." Things like worrying about a repeat of what happened between them fourteen years ago. And savoring her silky skin in case it did.

"I know what you mean," she said. "I can't seem to

turn my mind off either. I've got some issues that have me worried."

His attention immediately shifted to her. One sure-fire way to make sure Avery had no regrets was to take care of her every need, no matter how small.

"Like what?" he prompted.

She shifted next to him, tugging at the covers.

When she didn't say anything more, he gave her a nudge. "No judgment here. We can talk about anything." He grasped her hand, pressing a kiss to the palm. "Or we can *not* talk. It's up to you."

She squeezed his hand in return. "I have this meeting on Friday."

"You've mentioned that a time or two," he said, trying to remember if he'd heard who she'd gone to work for after leaving active duty. He couldn't come up with a name, although he was certain whatever company it was, they'd gotten a damned good employee. "If you like, you can run through your presentation or bounce ideas off me."

Avery kissed the underside of his chin. "Thanks, I might take you up on it. Besides the fact I want this contract more than I want to fit back into my favorite pair of jeans, I think my job's on the line."

Connor cupped her breast. "Only a fool would fail to see how competent you are." Or let her go after finally convincing her he could be trusted. He wanted to kick his younger self in the ass for letting their rivalry get so out of hand. Rolling her nipple between his thumb and finger, he asked, "Now that we have that settled, what else is keeping you awake?"

"Rob's getting married tomorrow," she said, just above a whisper.

Dumbass. Connor had known Robbie Gaffney since birth thanks to their families moving in the same circles. Growing up, the guy hadn't been that big of an ass. He'd been prone to brag about his family's money, but not coming anywhere near the shenanigans he pulled while Avery was deployed. What man in his right mind would ever look twice at another woman if he had Avery in his bed? Or tell her she didn't know how to please a man. Just in case she was still laboring under that fallacy, Connor drew her across his body till she straddled his hips. He brushed back hair that was spiraling around her head like an amber halo. "You do realize that you're better off without him."

"Yeah," she said, leaning down for a kiss.

He rolled them over. Arching over her, he nudged his cock into the apex of her thighs. "You want me to keep you distracted? Because I'd be really good at that."

Being this close to her played havoc with his goal of helping her with her issues. And the giggle she offered made it damned near impossible not to thrust inside her.

"You're very good at distractions, but his getting remarried isn't what's bothering me. He's up to something, and I can't figure out what it is."

As much as he wanted to pleasure all her worries into oblivion, Connor didn't want to downplay her concerns. Good pilots relied not only on what their instruments told them, but on their intuition as well. If Avery thought something was up, there probably was.

He switched on the bedside lamp. "Let's figure out what the dumbass is up to," he said.

"Sounds like a good idea for later." A wicked smile

formed on her lips. "Anything else you want to add to our agenda?" she asked, reaching for one of the condoms on the nightstand.

Yeah, figure out how to stretch two days into long-term.

****

Hours later, Avery slipped out of bed for a shower. After toweling off her hair, she pulled on a tank top and shorts. While Connor slept in the other room, she planned to catch up on her emails. That way when he woke, she could devote her full attention to him. She opened the door to find him awake. Resting on his side with his head propped up in his hand, he lay bare before her. God, to think she'd been up close and personal with that hard body of his. A smattering of dark hair covered his pecs. Below that, toned abs led her gaze south. As she walked toward the bed, Connor's erection grew.

Best. Compliment. Ever.

If nothing else positive came from her experience with Connor, she had to thank him for ridding her of Rob's lies. "Good morning," she said, crawling across the bed toward him. "How'd you sleep?"

"Like a well-satisfied man." He purred.

"What would you like to do today?" she asked. "Other than the obvious," she added, as she rubbed herself along his length.

He kissed her shoulder. "I need sustenance if I'm to keep up with you, Mad. How about breakfast on the balcony?"

Breakfast. *Damn*, she'd completely forgotten about having breakfast with the Collins family. She reached for the clock by the bed—nine. She couldn't remember the last time she'd slept that late. Avery scrambled off the bed. "I'm supposed to be having breakfast with Stephanie, Opie, and the kids downstairs now."

His brow knitted. "I've got some things on the boat I can take care of. We can meet up afterward if you like."

"Do that later," she told him. After the thorough way he'd rid her of her own insecurity, the last thing she wanted to do was make him think she regretted what they'd done. "I want you to come with me." Steph and Opie would be fine with learning she'd hooked up with Connor. After all, it was Stephanie who said she should have a vacation fling.

"Really?" he asked. "I wasn't sure…"

"Absolutely." She darted back for a quick kiss. "It's not like we can hole up in here till Friday." God, time was moving entirely too fast. In a little more than twenty-four hours her time with Connor would be over. Directly after her pitch, she was meeting Rob at the airport to pick up Will and then flying home to Atlanta.

Connor brushed back her hair and kissed his way up her neck. "Sounds like a plan, but I'll need a shower first." His blue eyes heated. "Care to join me?"

If she let herself get any more lost in their lust, they might not surface until sometime next week. "Tempting, but I better not." His lips did wicked things to her. "I'll catch up on some work while you shower."

Avery crossed to the other side of the suite and opened up her laptop. Minutes after pulling up the files containing her presentation, Connor's phone went off. Looking at the screen, the image of a teenaged girl and the name "Sofia" appeared. She let the call go to voicemail.

A short time later Connor opened the bathroom door. "Your niece called." Avery handed him the phone. "I wasn't sure what I should do."

He slid on the trousers he'd worn last night. "Thanks. I better see what's going on. She doesn't usually call unless she needs something."

She walked to the other room, but his deep voice carried. Even if she wasn't listening to the words, his patient tone revealed how much he loved the girl. Then when the anxiety in his voice grew, she also could tell he was in over his head. Nothing was trickier than helping a fifteen-year-old negotiate adolescence, especially with the added burden of grief.

When the call ended she handed him one of her *Flight Innovations* business cards. "I wrote my cell number on the back. I can't promise to have all the answers, but I do have some experience with the mystery that is the teen girl."

"Thanks," he said, accepting the card. As he read it, his face darkened.

Had she overstepped her bounds? "I know we said we were keeping things casual, but I thought you might like someone to talk to."

The muscles in his jaw ticked as seconds passed and he continued staring at her card.

"It's just an idea," she said, reaching for the glossy blue card that announced her title as Director of Marketing and Development. "I don't mean to suggest you don't know what you're doing." Or try to renegotiate their bargain.

He looked up. "No, it's fine. I can use all the help I can get." He moved to his wallet which he'd left by the television. "I'll just keep this here."

Something was definitely off, but if he wasn't ready to share, she wouldn't push.

Connor gestured toward the bedroom where the rest of his clothes lay on the floor. "Give me a couple minutes, and I'll be ready."

The uneasiness continued as they entered the elevator. As much as Avery wanted to press Connor for answers, now didn't seem to be the time. He put a hand to the small of her back as they walked through the hotel's lobby. The contact burned through her and eased some of her concerns about his sudden shift in attitude. Her relief was brief. After opening the door for her to the pool area, he let a gap grow between their bodies and even though it was no more than a few feet and most likely for the sake of propriety, it still felt like a huge chasm.

Striding ahead, she fixed a smile on her face. "I see you guys waited on me," she said as she took a seat at the table next to Stephanie.

"Like hogs to the trough," Opie replied. Seeing Connor, his eyes widened.

Avery braced for her two friends' reaction, especially when Connor drew up a chair from a nearby table and squeezed between her and Stephanie.

Stephanie broke the tension. "Coffee?" she asked, holding up a large French press.

"Good God, yes." She passed her cup over to Stephanie. Not that she needed any more stimulation with all the drama around her, but Avery was desperate for a distraction.

The adults busied themselves pretending to be absorbed with fruit and croissants at the table while Aiden and Diana chattered like magpies. With them present she doubted Steph or Opie would mention the elephant at the table—one more reason to love her godchildren. "So what do you guys have on tap today?"

Opie answered before his kids had a chance. "We're having a sandcastle building contest today." His eyes darted between Avery and Connor. "You?"

She shot a glance to Connor. Something cast a pall over his mood, making her wonder if he'd find a reason to leave. "I'm not sure."

He jerked his chin to the beach behind them. "I thought Avery and I would take my boat out for a few hours."

Avery. With that one sentence, her pulse soared. He'd used her name instead of her call sign. She liked the way it sounded on his lips. Then there was the other reason her palms were sweating. She had a secret she'd spent the past twenty years guarding. While it wasn't as embarrassing as revealing the intimate details of her failed marriage, it was a matter she wasn't anxious to have him find out. Her gaze darted to the marina where *The Nemesis* was tied up. If she confessed this little nugget of truth about herself, she'd never hear the end of it.

She scooted back her chair, her mind churning to come up with an alternative. "I've got some work I need to do first." In her haste to leave the table, she caught her foot on the chair leg.

"Easy, babe," Connor said as she tumbled in his lap. "We can take the boat out anytime you like." He tucked a strand of hair behind her ear.

Avery nodded, breaking the tether he had on her gaze. "Come up to my room when you're through with breakfast. We'll make our plans then."

****

Connor's attention followed Avery's retreating form. *I know we're just keeping things casual.* Her words echoed in his head. There was nothing casual about the way he felt about her. Never had been. From the moment he'd walked into the massage room yesterday, he'd been angling for a way to draw out their time together. All his plans were smashed like a pile of blocks under an angry toddler's foot when she handed him her business card. If she found out his company was in competition with hers, she'd never believe he hadn't planned this.

Turning to Opie and his crew he said, "Good to see you guys. Have a great time building those sandcastles." He headed for the path leading down to the beach, wanting to give Avery some time to work and him a minute to get his head screwed on straight.

He got as far as the gate when Opie called out, "Titan, hold up."

Connor stopped, knowing what Avery's wingman had to say before he even opened his mouth. Sure enough, as Connor turned around the guy's clenched jaw and narrowed eyes did his talking for him. He raised a finger. "Before you light into me, let me assure you Mad knows the score."

"She does, does she?" Opie crossed his arms. "And what is it?"

The realization that Avery stood between him and his goal of winning Carolina Entertainment's business twisted in his gut. It seemed a cruel joke that the two of them should once again be pitted against one another. If Connor hadn't just had a fresh taste of what it would be like with her, he might have had the strength to walk away. It would be the right thing to do. The feel of her skin burned too hot for him ignore. "This is strictly casual. No emotions involved."

Opie threw his arms up in frustration. "Man, I thought you'd changed. I can't believe you'd treat Mad Dog like that despite your past."

Connor clenched his fists. Maybe he hadn't played things by the numbers early in his career, but all those years he and Mad Dog had vied for the choicest positions he'd treated her as an equal. A worthy advisory who'd earned his respect. To offer anything less than his best would be an insult. "What happened back in the day has no bearing on this. In fact, we've put that all behind us. Mad and I are two adults having a few days' fun. That's it."

"And when Friday rolls around?" Opie asked.

Just the thought of it felt like a knife in his chest. He rubbed his sternum. "She goes her way, and I go mine. None the worse for wear." That last bit was a blatant lie. It had taken him years to get where he could remember the first time he'd made love to Avery without regret firing in his chest. He'd probably go to his grave hurting after this week.

Opie stabbed a finger at Connor. "See to it that you keep that promise. Avery's a good and decent person, and she deserves better than—"

"Than me," Connor interjected. "Yeah, she does." She deserved someone who could offer years instead of days, who'd be in her corner instead of her constant opponent. "Like I said, she knows what she's getting herself into."

****

Moments after Avery reached her hotel room, a rap

came on the door. Doubling back, she didn't bother to look through the peephole. She'd been friends with Stephanie long enough to know the woman wasn't fooled by her and Connor's poolside charade. "I know what I'm doing," she said by way of greeting.

Stephanie rolled her eyes as she stepped inside the room. "Do you now?" She shook her head like Avery announced she quit her job to be a pole dancer. "I said you should have a fling. I didn't know I needed to specify that it should be with someone you actually *liked*."

"I like him just fine," she said, fighting to keep the amusement out of her voice.

Stephanie's brow arched. "Since when?"

Avery plopped at one end of the suite's sofa and patted the adjacent cushion. Once Stephanie took the spot next to her, she began her explanation. "We had dinner last night. He's different from how he was a couple years ago," she said, still surprised at how much he'd changed since their navy days.

"I doubt that," Steph said, a skeptical grimace on her face. "You know what they say about leopards."

Yesterday she would have agreed, but that was before she'd learned his reputation as a maverick barely scratched the surface of him as a man. "Did you know he resigned his commission in order to raise his niece and take over his family's business?"

Stephanie's eyes widened. "I didn't." She cocked her head, her brow furrowing. "So are you two a thing now?"

Avery shrugged. "On Friday he'll go his way, I'll go mine."

After last night, the idea of leaving him left a

hollow ache in her heart. What should have been nothing more than two adults enjoying a good time together, weighed on her now.

Her thoughts rewound to their days at the Academy and the first time they'd made love. It was more than sex back then too, which scared her eighteen-year-old self. Guilt tore at her heart for hurting him back then, even as she wondered if perhaps this time it would be *her* heart that got broken.

Stephanie let out a breath. "Be careful," she chided as she stood and walked to the door.

"Aren't I always?" Avery hugged her friend. "I'll call you next week when I get back to Atlanta."

With her friend gone, she padded over to the table she used as a desk and pulled up the computer file containing her pitch. She stared at the presentation for several seconds before pushing her laptop aside. Too many thoughts fought for attention to settle on one concern. Instead of diving into work like she ought, she reached for her phone. A quick check-in with Will would ease some of the worry churning in her stomach. Then she could focus on the emerging issues at hand— discovering what darkened Connor's mood earlier and keeping him from learning she'd rather be beat with a stick than take a ride on his boat.

****

In the lobby, Connor watched the bank of elevators, his thoughts on the conversation he'd had with Opie. He'd assured Avery's wingman that the two of them knew the score. Too bad he was having a hard time convincing himself. His phone vibrated in his pocket. He swore under his breath when he checked the screen. For a morning that started with such promise, it was rolling downhill fast. "What's up, Hillary?" he asked his office manager.

"The price of aviation fuel," she quipped. "Have you heard from Carolina Entertainment?"

The elevator doors opened, and he stepped inside. "Not yet, but we won't know anything until the other companies have made their presentations."

"I know, but what does your gut say?"

His gut told him with Avery pitching the rival company's bid, his chances were at best even money. It didn't matter if she was flying or shooting pool, she always brought her A game.

Then again, so did he. Like her, a lot rode on the success of their respective presentations. "We're definitely in the running." Even before he'd found out who was heading up the competition's pitch, he'd written his bid to be competitive. But was it good enough?

"Any chance you can sweeten the deal or get some inside information on what the competitors are offering?" Hillary asked. "I don't need to remind you that we need this if we're to make next month's payroll."

"I know." He also still had thousands left to repay on the loan Stephen had taken out to finance his drug habit. Then there was the money he needed to put aside for Sofia's college tuition. The money he'd get from selling his boat would finish paying off the investors Stephen had stolen from but would leave very little for operating expenses. And nothing to see to Sofia's future.

By the time he finished the conversation with his office manager, he'd reached Avery's room. Earlier they'd stopped by the hotel front desk where she requested an extra room key. He let himself in with it, anxious to escape reality for a while. As he stepped inside, he caught sight of a long leg propped on the balcony railing against the backdrop of blue sky and water. He drew nearer. Tucking her phone between her ear and shoulder, she released her hair from the ponytail. As it tumbled down her bare shoulders, it made him half-crazy to run his fingers through it.

"I'm glad you're having a good time." Avery spoke to someone on the phone.

Connor stayed inside the sliding glass door to give her privacy. She had mentioned wanting to talk to her son. Pulling up a chair to wait, his gaze landed on the document open on the computer screen—her pitch to Carolina Entertainment. His fingers itched to arrow the page down to get a better look. He only needed a quick peek at the bottom line. If hers was better, he could undercut the deal thus ensuring Aviation Options stayed afloat.

He groaned, hating himself for even entertaining the thought…but thirty people relied on him for their livelihood. No pressure there. Before, he wouldn't have given a second thought to doing whatever it took to come out on top. But he'd experienced the painful effects of cheating, thanks to Stephen's embezzlement. This was Avery he was dealing with, so there really was no decision. He wouldn't do anything to hurt her— regardless of the consequences.

He stood, needing to eliminate temptation. As he closed the lid on her laptop, she opened the slider and stepped into the room. "Everything okay with Will?" he asked.

"Yeah." Her narrowed gaze darted between him and her laptop. "He's getting ready for the wedding."

Connor crossed the room, taking her in his arms. With the hours together growing short, he wanted her all to himself. No well-meaning friends, intruding work issues, only the two of them. "Are you ready to go out on my boat for a couple hours?"

When she didn't answer immediately, he backed them toward the bed intent on using a little persuasion. "You can take your phone if you're worried about Will," he said, peppering kisses along her jaw.

"I need to prep for my meeting," she said, pointing to her computer.

"That's not until tomorrow, plenty of time."

She thrust her hips against him, grinding against his erection. "You wouldn't rather stay in here?"

He would have considered the option except for two things. First, he needed to put some distance between him and her computer. If Avery ever learned his company had competed against hers, even if she eventually won the contract, he'd never convince her he hadn't cook up this whole affair in order to once again best her. Second, the little fantasy his sleeping brain conjured up last night played on constant rewind.

"I had a very naughty dream that involved making love to you on the deck of my boat," he told her. "I'll let you drive if you like." He rolled them so that she was on top. "I know how you like to be in charge."

"You win," she said, chuckling. "But don't get too used to it."

Chapter Eight

Anxiety prickled Avery's scalp as she stared at the gap between *The Nemesis* and the dock. It seemed yards across instead of inches. Connor leaped across then held out a hand for her. *I can do this.* If she could survive water training, she'd survive this. "Permission to come aboard, Captain," she said, feigning lightness she didn't feel.

A broad smile creased his face. "Permission granted, wench. Now get your scurvy ass over here."

Picturing herself already in his arms, she propelled her body across the gap. Relief loosened the knot in her stomach as he caught her and pulled her in close.

"Welcome aboard," he said. He pressed a hungry kiss to her lips, his hand sliding down to her bottom.

When the kiss ended he asked, "Would you like a tour?"

She scanned *The Nemesis's* deck. A small seating area made of crisp blue cushions and a low table filled the boat's aft section. Shiny chrome gunwales topped the bulkhead, with a windscreen protecting the captain's chair and wheel.

Then she zeroed in on the doors leading below deck as if they led to the Promised Land. "Absolutely." Perhaps if she couldn't see the water that seemed dark enough to hide a dozen hungry sharks, she'd be able to enjoy the beautiful boat and its handsome captain.

After unfastening the hatch, he motioned for her to descend the steeply angled stairs ahead of him. Below deck she was again taken with the boat's luxurious finishing. A bank of cabinets, small appliances, and sink made up the portside galley, while a banquette of ivory cushions and a teak table flanked the starboard side.

Pointing to a narrow corridor, he said, "The head is the door on the left, if you need it."

"Thanks."

Coming up from behind, he wrapped her with thick arms. Then he kissed her shoulder. "As you can see the other is the stateroom," he said, indicating the partially open door through which she could see the corner of a suede-covered berth.

Maybe she could convince him they could reenact his dream while still anchored at the marina. Turning in his embrace, she made a go for his belt.

He stilled her hand. "As much as I'm looking forward to christening *The Nemesis,* I thought we'd take her out on the water first."

She drew in a breath. This was her putting on her big girl panties. "Sure."

"I need to finish tuning the engine, and we can leave," he said as he reached for the hatch at their feet. "You can keep me company or relax topside while I do it."

She lowered herself to the deck very content to watch while he worked, especially after he pulled off his shirt. "I didn't know you could repair boats. You really do have a lot of hidden talents."

"It's not that hard," he said, reaching for a wrench from the large leather bag he'd hauled up from the engine compartment. "It's the same internal combustion engine as a car." His contented smile demonstrated his affection for the boat.

"How long have you had her?"

"My old man gave her to me as a high school graduation present."

"Wow," she said, her eyebrows arching. "That beats the luggage my folks gave me."

He laughed darkly. "At the time I thought it was pretty cool too. I mean, who wouldn't be psyched about getting a yacht. It took a couple years for me to figure out it was my father's way of telling me to beat it—that I needn't expect a place in the company. He had the heir and didn't need a spare hanging around."

"God, Titan, that's harsh."

"I got over it," he said with a shrug. "Despite the subtle message my dad was trying to send, *The Nemesis* means the world to me. I can take her out on the water and every concern in the world just drifts away."

"That's beautiful," she said, surprised that anyone could forgive such cruelty.

Connor blew out a breath. "But it looks like I might have to sell her if my company's finances don't improve. My brother left the family business in rough shape."

"Oh, I'm sorry," she said, focusing on a face that hid nothing. His eyes spoke of regret and yearning even as the corners of his mouth relayed a tenderness she hadn't expected.

"No need to feel sorry. Thankfully, Bash has expressed an interest in buying her if it comes to that." He turned back to his work.

"But you love this boat, and having to give her up

to fix a problem you didn't create must be a bitter pill to swallow."

"Doing the right thing isn't always pleasant or easy." He smiled. "Maybe playing the good guy for once will bank me a little karma for a rainy day."

Her gaze latched onto lips that looked like they could devour a woman and make her glad for it. Had he changed or had she seen what she wanted to find all those years ago? Either way the person in front of her was nothing like the man she'd supposed him to be. Even his appearance had changed. Dark curls that nearly touched his collar replaced the closely cropped hair from their navy days. This Connor seemed gentle, humble—infinitely more lovable. She thumbed at his whiskers, remembering the delicious rasp of his goatee against her skin. "And who doesn't need a little karma in the bank," she said, hoping life repaid his sacrifice.

For the next several minutes he tinkered with the boat's engine, their only conversation requests for her to pass him tools, until finally he dropped a wrench in his tool bag. "All done," he said, wiping his hands on a nearby rag. "Let's go topside. I'm dying to get you out on the open water." A wicked grin flashed across his face, reminding her that not everything about him had changed. The cocky, sexy aviator was never more than a smart-ass remark away.

She followed him topside and immediately her pulse kicked up a notch. "Um, where are the PFDs?" she asked, looking around.

He scooted past her to grab the mooring lines that held the boat to the dock. "Under the bench," he said, thumbing over his shoulder.

She made for the life preservers like another

woman might go for a designer bag at a fifty percent off sale. In a pair of seconds she pulled the orange vest out of the compartment.

"You don't need to wear one. The Coast Guard's not reporting rough weather until late tonight. We'll be back on land before then."

"Safety first," she said, pulling it over her head. As she fastened the straps and settled into a seat, she felt like the biggest baby. She'd been ejected into twenty feet of frigid water, expected to work her way out of a parachute harness, and then tread water for ten minutes. All she had to do now was sit in the sun and feel the spring breeze against her face.

He cast off the ropes then moved to the wheel. "All set?" he asked, smiling as he gave her a quick peck.

Sitting across from him in a chair she wished had a seatbelt, Avery white knuckled the gunwales. "Absolutely," she lied, fixing her gaze on the shoreline. It helped a little until the distance between her and it grew too far for her to swim. Then she trained her attention on the handsome man whose strong arms and chiseled features kept her imagination from conjuring up worst case scenarios. When he opened up the throttle and the boat began to pitch against the waves, she clenched her eyelids to shut out the water rushing past her. The reduction in sensory input did little to lessen her anxiety. With the spray stinging her face and the scent of seawater filling her nose, the memory of the childhood incident that caused her fear played in an endless loop in her brain. Avery fought against the tide of panic, opening her eyes skyward to take in the endless blue she loved so much.

A century later, he cut the engine and the boat

settled to a gentle rock. Turning to her he said, "Hey babe, you're looking a little green around the gills."

Her answer had to work its way past the bile in her throat. "Just a little seasick," she said, offering him a wan smile.

He quirked an eyebrow, evidently seeing through her lie. As a pilot she was accustomed to air turbulence in addition to banked turns and deep dives. In light of the secrets he'd already learned about her, admitting her fear seemed like a nonevent. She drew in a breath. "I hate the water."

He looked at her like she told him she was allergic to air. "I went through survival training with you. You do not."

"Oh, but I do." She held out her shaking hand. "Does this look like someone who's having fun to you?" Part of her still feared he'd burst out laughing or start in on a round of ego-bruising teasing. Instead he crossed to her side of the boat and wrapped an anchoring arm around her. He really wasn't the man she'd always thought he was, and it made her want more than the few days they'd agreed to more than she wanted off that boat.

He took her hand and kissed her fingers one by one. "I gotta ask," he said with only the tiniest bit of humor in his voice. "Why'd you join the Navy if you hate the water?"

The irony of her career choice wasn't lost on her. Her biggest reason for bucking family tradition was to escape her father's legacy. General Madigan cast a large shadow, and she'd been certain at eighteen she'd never escape it in the army. The rank she'd achieved was due to her hard work, not her family name. She'd also come to love the navy even if she didn't enjoy certain aspects of it. Besides in nine years, she'd never ejected from a plane. "Like you, my goal as an aviator is to stay *out* of the water."

"Jeez, Mad," he said, raking his fingers through his hair. "Why didn't you say something?"

She did sound a little silly now for not speaking up. "I didn't think it would be this bad. Plus, I wanted to give you your fantasy."

"You didn't have to do that." He tugged her into his lap. "You're my fantasy. Always have been."

Now that he knew all her idiosyncrasies—her insecurities about sex and fear of the water—she figured there wasn't any point in holding back. "Does that mean you might be interested in doing away with our little deadline?"

His eyes sparked as he cupped her chin. "You'd want that—us trying the commuter relationship thing?"

Her heart hammered in her chest. She had no idea how they'd work around distance and their family commitments, but she had to see if they could make a go of it. "If you are."

"Oh, hell yeah," he said, pulling her down for a deep kiss. "In the meantime, how about we act out that dream I had this morning."

****

Later, as the afternoon sun caressed Avery's bare back and her head rested against Connor's chest, concerns about delicate areas getting sunburned barely flickered through her sated brain. In fact, little other than the feel of his hard muscles against her cheek occupied her thoughts. She was even enjoying the boat's gentle rocking. When a stiff breeze sent an unexpected chill across her skin, she nestled deeper into his embrace.

Connor sat up, bringing her with him. With a hand shielding his eyes, he scanned the skies to the west. "Let's head back. It looks as if the front is coming in ahead of schedule." He scooted from underneath her and reached to the deck for his shorts and T-shirt. After pulling them on, he trailed a hand lazily up her leg. "I don't want to undo all the progress you've made because I definitely want to do this again."

Progress. The word seemed too simplistic to describe the changes that occurred during the past couple days, and not just because he'd gotten her on the water. It seemed her life was headed in a positive direction for the first time in years.

Still languid from the sun and sex, it took her a moment to muster the will to move. She propped her cheek against her palm and watched with an appreciative eye as he took the captain's seat. His shoulders were broader than she remembered, and his once arrogant persona had mellowed. He glanced over his shoulder, catching her staring. With a wink he asked, "What's got you smiling like you just learned a juicy secret?"

"You." She pulled on her shorts and tank top, then crossed the deck, noting how it pitched under her feet. "Thanks for not making fun of me," she said, wrapping an arm around him.

"I wouldn't dare," he chuckled. He took her hands in his. "In fact, I'm more than a little impressed at your bravery."

Remembering the sweet way they'd made love, she said, "It was worth—" A yawn cut off the rest of her sentence.

"You could go below and take a nap if you like," he said, cupping the back of her head and bringing her in for a kiss. "I'll wake you when we get back to the marina."

A nap sounded perfect, especially as two-foot swells began buffeting the boat. "I think I'll take you up on that."

As she pulled from his embrace, Connor reached for the ignition button on the console. An anemic sputter stopped her from heading below. "She's just being temperamental," he said waving her on. "I'll have her going in just a sec."

Having seen his mechanical skills in action hours earlier, she took the ladder below deck with only the tiniest knot in her stomach. By the time she reached the stateroom, she was too drowsy to follow through with the worry about *The Nemesis's* engine. She curled up on his bed, tugging the comforter to her chin. As sleep overtook her, she heard the thud of Connor opening the panel to the engine room.

****

"Avery," Connor whispered some time later. He shook her gently. "We have a little problem."

"What?" she asked, levering upright. Her wide eyes raked over him. "What's wrong?"

He hated the tension registering on her beautiful face, especially since he'd helped put it there. "The engine blew a gasket, and I don't have the parts here to fix it."

"Okay?" she said. "Is that a minor annoyance type problem, or a Houston-we-have-a- problem, problem?"

He sat down on the edge of the berth. "Between the

storm and night coming on, it will be morning before the towing company can get to us."

She clenched her eyes. "Jeez, and we're stuck out here in the open ocean like lightning rods." As if on cue, thunder rumbled in the distance and the boat began pitching in the water. Avery gripped the comforter.

"I'm so sorry, babe. If I'd known…" He pulled her into him. Her warm breath tickled his neck as she struggled to control her fear.

She cringed as another clap of thunder followed quickly on the heels of a too-close-for-comfort lightning strike. "I need something to keep my mind off the storm," she said, her voice thin and reedy.

Connor trailed a hand down her back to cup her bottom. Well, if that's what she needed, he could do that all night long. "Did you have something in mind?"

"Actually, I do," she said, pulling back so he caught the pleading in her gaze. "Would you listen to me practice my pitch? If I'm not worried about blowing the presentation tomorrow, that would be at least one less thing to worry about."

If he were anything but a selfish bastard, he'd tell her everything. It was the right thing to do despite the risk of harming their fragile relationship. The confession perched on the end of his lips. Instead, he made a last ditch effort to distract her by nibbling the tender spot behind her ear. "Can't I get you to consider another thought-diverting option?" he crooned.

"Stop." She laughed as she pushed against his chest. "Who's the sex-crazed monster now?"

"I think I have a deck of cards in the galley if you're not up for more hanky-panky," he said, grasping for options. It wasn't that he didn't want to help her. He still didn't trust himself with the details of her company's offering to Carolina Entertainment.

"Tempting," she chuckled, scooting back against the headboard. "Let me run through it once just to be sure I haven't forgotten it."

"You have it all memorized?" he asked, smiling at his overachieving lover.

She nodded. "You bet. After the disaster of my first sales pitch, I've never left anything to chance." She grimaced. "Which makes me even more anxious about being stuck out here in the middle of the ocean."

"I'm sorry. If I'd had any idea the gasket was on its last leg, I never would have taken us out."

"It's not your fault," she countered. "Besides, the tug boat will be here bright and early in the morning to take us back."

"You bet," he said, praying to Poseidon that nothing else prevented them from getting back to shore. Though he'd set the anchor, it wasn't out of the realm of possibilities the gusts of wind that buffeted the boat could move them off the coordinates he'd given the towboat captain. "Now let me hear this stellar pitch," he said, plastering on a smile.

At the end of her eight-minute speech, he didn't know whether to cheer or call Bash to see if the guy was still interested in buying his boat. Back at the bar he'd dismissed the offer out of hand, but given the strength of her pitch it might prove to be a lifeline. Either way, he couldn't help being impressed. "Fantastic," he said, paying respect where it was due. There was still a sliver of chance Carolina Entertainment would choose his company. While Flight Innovations' bid offered a few perks his company couldn't, Aviation Option's bottom line was better.

"Thanks," she said. "Now where's that deck of cards?" She eased past him, scooting into the galley. Then she tucked herself into the banquette while he scrounged in the junk drawer. She took the deck from him, and he slipped into the other side of the bench seat like a man who'd lost the will to live.

"What?" she asked, taking note of his less than enthusiastic response to her latest diversion tactic. "Are you not up for a little friendly competition?"

He pulled his thoughts from visions of what would happen if he didn't get the contract. "Do your worst," he said, enjoying the grin on her face. It wasn't as much fun as making love, but what could it hurt to play a few hands of gin rummy.

"Have you ever played war?"

He quirked an eyebrow. "Sure. Sofia and I used to play before she got too grown to hang out with her uncle."

She rubbed her hands together. "This is a variation on that game. Winner gets to ask the loser a question which he has to answer truthfully."

The last thing he was in the position to do was tell the truth. He hid the dread coiling in his stomach behind a smile and a pithy comeback. "*He*," he emphasized. "That assumes it won't be you having to answer my penetrating queries."

She jutted out her chin. "Do your worst. After you found out my past issues with Rob and my little water phobia, my life is an open book." She shuffled the deck with a practiced hand and quickly dealt the cards. "Ready, set, go," she said, laying down a four of diamonds to his two of clubs.

"Why have you never married?" she asked too quickly not to have had that one in her back pocket for a while.

"Jeez, what's with the heavy questions?" he teased as he bought himself some time. "I was expecting something like, what was my favorite color." He caught her gaze. "It's gray, by the way." When her brow furrowed, he clarified. "The color of your eyes."

"Oh." A lovely blush colored her cheeks. "Let's go again," she said, her smile revealing a dimple.

This time his jack of hearts beat her eight of spades. "What's your favorite part of this week?" he asked, still hoping to redirect her thoughts to safer, more sensual topics.

"Fishing for compliments, I see." She cocked her head. "I don't know. I hope it hasn't happened yet," she said, a small smile playing at her lips. Then she threw down a king of spades that trumped his nine of diamonds. "I win," she squealed.

"Competitive much?" *God, if only all their competition was this fun.*

"Yes," she said bouncing in her seat as she scooped up both cards. "You are too, so don't act like you don't want to come out on top."

Connor reached across the table to run his finger up her arm. "I definitely love topping you."

Avery rolled her eyes. "Let's see," she said, tapping her finger to her lips. "Tell me about your family's business."

A fissure of anxiety tightened his gut. The type of business he ran was the last thing he wanted her to find out. If he so much as offered the name of his company, she'd begin to connect the dots. "That's not a question.

Let's go again," he said, throwing down an eight of spades.

She pushed the card back in his direction. "What is this, *Jeopardy?* I'll rephrase the question."

In a Hail Mary attempt at redirection he said, "You know, I never did answer your first question."

Her gaze bored into him, as if she could see through all the layers of arrogance, charm, and bullshit down to his very soul. "Okay. Why has some sweet young thing never caught your eye?"

He hoped the sound of rain hitting the deck was enough to drown out the racket his heart was making. He'd trade a truth that would show how much he'd wanted her all these years and risk revealing what a sap he was, for a revelation that could end everything that was within his grasp. "I never wanted to settle for second best, and the woman I wanted hated me on sight."

Several heartbeats ticked past with only the sound of water lapping against the hull filling the tension-thick air. "I never hated you, really." She bit her lip. "I didn't know how to handle my feelings for you, so I channeled them into feeding our rivalry."

"You're not the only one who let pride get in the way. I deserved a lot of your animosity. For years, I believed if I proved to my old man what a good aviator I was, I'd finally get some of the golden glory he heaped on my brother, Stephen." He shook his head at the foolishness of it all. Despite his brother's shenanigans with Aviation Options' money, their father had been unwilling to hear a word against the heir apparent.

"Will you tell me about Sofia?" she asked, sliding

around to nestle against him. "I want to hear about this girl who has you wrapped around her little finger."

Connor draped his arm around her shoulders, drawing her close to his side. "She's not the only one." *God, where to start?* Nothing in his life prepared him for parenting a grieving preteen. "I don't mind telling you the first year after her dad died I wasn't sure either one of us would survive." His heart ached remembering the angry, frightened girl. Their saving grace had been counseling. "We're in a pretty good place now. Although I never know in the mornings if I'll see sweet Sofia or the sullen teen who'd just as soon bite my head off as to look at me. She's a good kid," he continued then had to clear the emotion from his throat. "Every now and then I catch a glimpse of the brilliant young woman she'll be in a few years."

"She sounds like a wonderful young lady," she said, giving his hand a squeeze.

"I have an idea," he said, giving voice to a plan he'd thought up while the two of them dozed topside. It might be too much too soon, but he wanted to show her he wanted more than a few stolen weekends. When Avery made an agreeable noise, he gave it a shot. "We talked a little about you spending weekends that Will is with his dad down here with me. I'd also like you to bring him with you the first chance you get." He kissed the top of her head. "I'm hoping this is leading somewhere, and I want the kids to get to know each other."

"I'd like that a lot." Avery tilted her head up. "Hey, it sounds like the storm is over."

"Would you like to go topside and see the stars? This far out at sea, we should get a pretty good show."

Their arms linked, they stepped up onto the rain-soaked deck. He didn't know what Avery would classify as her favorite part of their time together, but with his arms wrapped around her and her perfume filling his senses, right now ranked top of his list for the week. Perhaps even in the last twenty years. Dare he hope that by some miracle he could hold onto Avery and keep his business afloat?

Chapter Nine

Connor scanned the horizon as the sun peeked over the water. Its rays reflected off the surface, making it look like a million floating crystals. If he ignored the doom-predicting voices in his head, it would have been a perfect morning. The sky above his boat was azure and the swells below gentle. Between the two lay Avery—the woman he loved. Not loved—as in admired, respected, or lusted after. Loved—as in irretrievably altered—loved. The realization came to him during the night while she'd slept in his arms. The echo of that truth still made his chest ache.

He wanted forever with this woman. It seemed a cruel twist of fate that after coming to terms with his feelings for her, that they once again found themselves as rivals. He clenched his fists in frustration. If only he could keep her from finding out.

His conscience pricked him. Connor should have told her what he knew last night when she'd practiced her pitch, but his emotions made him selfish as well as cautious. There was much more at stake now than in the past. He couldn't risk her finding out until he had a chance to make her fall in love with him. Top of that to-do list was taking care of her needs, and right now she needed to be back onshore in time for her pitch.

"Beautiful morning, isn't it," she said, slipping up behind him.

Connor tilted his head to capture her mouth with his. "Better now that you're up. How'd you sleep?"

"Great." She stole the mug of coffee from his hand and took a sip.

That simple act of intimacy stirred him, and he tugged her onto his embrace. "There's more of that downstairs."

"Maybe later," she said, nuzzling into his neck. She shielded her eyes as she looked westward. "How far out do you think we are?"

"The anchor didn't hold as I'd feared. I checked my instruments and it looks like we're further south from Wilmington and about two and a half miles out."

She nodded. "I thought we were pretty far out since when I checked my phone I didn't have a signal."

"I was able to radio the tug service."

"And?" she prompted.

"We weren't the only ones to get caught off guard by that thunderstorm. The Coast Guard has asked for the tow company to help with a search and rescue. When I radioed in our new coordinates, they let me know we were on the schedule, but it might be late afternoon before they could get to us."

She dropped her chin to her chest.

"I'm so sorry," he told her. "Keep checking your phone for a signal. If we drift into the current, it might bring us within cell range."

She let out a breath. "That still doesn't get me to my meeting."

He racked his brain for a way around this situation. "Maybe Mr. Pres…," he began before catching himself. "Maybe the guy you're pitching to will let you reschedule." Even as he made the suggestion, he doubted Charles Preston would be willing to do so.

Connor had had two meetings with Carolina Entertainment's vice president prior to his own pitch Monday. None of the encounters led him to believe the guy was anything other than a hard ass. Preston stated that he wanted the proposals out of the way and the contract awarded ASAP. Whichever company won the contract was expected to begin transporting the entertainers in a little over a week.

"I'm keeping my fingers crossed," she said, even though her tone of voice was anything but hopeful. "But if I don't make the appointment, I'll be making a really unpleasant call to my boss."

Connor eased away from her. "Let me see if I can get the tow company to put us at the top of the list."

****

Avery stretched and yawned, her first impulse after waking from her nap to reach for her phone. The sight of the little pyramid at the corner sent her spirits soaring. At least now she could finally let Mr. Preston know what had happened.

Two hours after Connor radioed the tug company, they were still waiting. He'd even tried finding other boats that'd be willing to come pick her up—without success. When that failed, he'd gone below and begun tinkering with the engine.

Rather than watch impotently, she made breakfast. Then she took a book she found tucked in a cupboard in Connor's stateroom and headed topside. She'd curled up on the cushions where they'd made love the day before, hoping Connor would take the hint and join her. When he didn't, she picked up her phone.

Just as she was about to punch in Preston's

number, a flash of light caught her attention. In the distance off the port side of the boat, were the tops of hotels. "Connor, come here," she shouted. "I see the shore."

The metallic thunk of tools hitting wood was followed by his head popping over the deck. "Well, what do you know, I guess we drifted into the current," he said, shielding his eyes.

She visually measured the distance, figuring it to be a couple hundred yards. "Do you think it'll take us any closer?"

His gaze shifted between their position and the shore. "It's possible," he said. "But without a dingy, we're still SOL."

She looked over the side of the boat. "How deep do you think the water is here?"

"This far out," Connor said with a shrug. "It could be several hundred feet."

A shiver crawled through her. Although, really what did it matter? Ten feet or ten thousand feet, it was all cold, dark, and filled with predators who probably would mistake her fair skin for the underbelly of a tasty treat.

Connor rubbed the goose bumps that dotted her arms. "The tow company will be here before nightfall. Why don't you call your client and see if he'll reschedule for tomorrow."

"At this point, I think it's my only option," she said, tapping out Carolina Entertainment's number. Five minutes later Avery's stomach was in knots. "I understand, Mr. Preston. Thank you for your understanding. You won't be sorry."

She stowed the phone in the pocket of her shorts,

her phone call having earned her a two-hour extension. "He's agreed to stay until five. He has a wedding to go to tonight, and then he's flying out in the morning. Mine is the last pitch he'll hear. He's making his decision tonight before he leaves for the west coast."

Connor gripped her upper arms, squeezing gently. "You have to know…"

"It isn't your fault any more than it's mine," she assured him. But she doubted her boss would take that under consideration. Her thoughts shot back to the last conversation with her boss. He'd conveyed in every way possible—short of coming straight out and saying so—that her future at Flight Innovations rode on her getting Mr. Preston to put ink to paper.

Fear of losing her job sent pinpricks of anxiety dancing across her scalp. She had a couple weeks' salary saved up, but that wouldn't be enough to keep a roof over her and Will's head, especially since Rob was as consistent with child support as she was at sticking to a diet.

The need to take charge of the situation had her reaching far out of her comfort zone for options. She looked out over the end of the boat. In the past few minutes they'd drifted further along the coast but no closer to shore. She couldn't wait and hope the tow company got to them in time.

She drew in a breath. "I'm swimming it," she said, throwing her legs over the side.

He caught her around the waist. "Have you lost your mind?" he growled as he hauled her back inside the boat. "That's more than two hundred yards."

"Yeah, I probably have," she said, burying her face into his chest. "But I have to try."

Connor pulled back, his dark eyes studying her for a moment as if testing her resolve. "I'm going with you," he finally said.

Avery shook her head. There was no sense in him risking his boat. "No. You can't afford to let *The Nemesis* run aground on a sand bar." She shared her plan as it came to her. "When I get to shore, I'll walk to one of the hotels and call a cab."

"What about your computer and some dry clothes?" he asked, proving she still needed his help even if he didn't actually make the swim with her.

"I have the presentation memorized, remember. As for my attire, I have to hope Mr. Preston will see that I'm willing to do whatever it takes to close the deal."

No, I won't let you do this," he said, catching her as she reached for the gunwale again. "It's not worth the risk."

Frustration had her jerking out of his hold. "You don't get to make that decision for me." Hearing the harshness in her voice, and seeing the hurt on Connor's face, she explained. "It's more than just this contract, or even my job. I won't be held prisoner by my fears. I never have before, and I won't now."

Determination flared in his eyes as he met her gaze. "Not without me you won't."

It looked like she'd met her match in the stubbornness department. "Suit yourself."

Five minutes later, after they'd informed the tow company of the new plan and stowed their cell phones and wallets in waterproof bags, she was glad his hard-headedness matched her own. She gripped his hand as the two of them slipped over the edge of the boat.

After a quick baptism, Avery surfaced thanks to the

personal flotation device, and the two of them began swimming toward the beach. "I'm right here," he assured her, keeping her within arms' reach. "We'll take this slowly."

She nodded, taking courage in his calm voice and easy strokes that cut through the water. But even as she nodded, a wave washed over her, choking her with salty water. It burned her throat and stung her eyes. In a flash she was in the muddy north Georgia lake that lay at the root of her fear. The eight-year-old girl still inside her after all these years panicked, and a wave pushed her below the surface.

Connor gripped the collar of her PFD. "I got you," he said as she sputtered and choked. "But you've got to keep moving."

What had she been thinking? An unemployed mom was better than a dead one. "I can't." Another wave washed over her. "I quit." She choked out the words.

"You can quit when you get to the shore." His voice came as a low growl.

They struggled together against the waves, making impossibly slow progress. After a few yards, her arms burned with fatigue. She rolled over and began backstroking her way toward shore. "Need help?" he asked.

She couldn't let him do her work for her. "I'm good," she said, beginning to stroke her way through the water. "I just needed to catch my breath." Finally, as she bobbed along the top of a wave, she caught sight of sunbathers lounging on the sand in front of a hotel. Optimism soared only to come crashing down as she felt the unmistakable tug of an undertow.

She eyed the beach with more longing than she'd

ever given a piece of chocolate. In order to escape the undertow, they had to drift parallel to shore before they could close the gap. When her arms were burning with fatigue as much as her eyes and throat were from swallowing seawater, she began making promises to God.

She'd no more said her silent "amen" than Connor told her, "Reach down with your feet. You can touch now."

The bottom felt heavenly even as the loose bottom shifted and a few shells dug into her feet. She dogpaddled through the waves and then collapsed onto the beach. Fisting the sand and drawing air into her lungs, triumph filled her soul and made her giddy. "I'm never getting in the water again."

****

Twenty minutes later the taxi pulled inside the hotel portico and Avery stepped from the curb to meet it. Connor reached the rear door first and opened it for her. "Call me when you're done."

Nerves bubbled up inside her. "Come with," she requested, tugging his hand. He was her rudder during the storm the night before and her wingman while she followed through on the crazy idea to swim to shore.

"You'll be fine," he said, offering her a smile. Then a dark expression crossed his face. "You don't need me there."

"Please," she said, pleading with her eyes.

He let out a breath but climbed in beside her. As they took off toward Wilmington, she checked the time on her phone. Unless some other disaster befell them, she'd make it in time. She even would be making her presentation in dry clothes, due to Connor's clear thinking.

"Thanks for the dress," Avery said, brushing her hand across the bright pink and orange fabric.

The corner of his mouth turned up. "Sorry there wasn't anything more suitable in the hotel's gift shop."

She took a sip from the water bottle he'd also snagged for her while she'd been arranging for a taxi. The cool water soothed her throat, still rough thanks to the gallon of seawater she'd swallowed. "It beats turning up looking like a drowned rat."

She closed her eyes and tried to remember the first line of her pitch. Drawing a blank, panic flared in her stomach. "Crap, I can't remember what type of aircraft we're supplying."

"Beech Jet 400," he supplied. "And you're offering one flight attendant for every ten people, and availability guaranteed with six hours' notice."

"I'd be up cripple creek if it weren't for you," she said, squeezing his hand.

The muscles in his jaw ticked. "You wouldn't be in this position if it weren't for me."

"It's not like you broke your boat on purpose," she said, hoping to assuage his misplaced guilt.

He nodded briskly, and they made the rest of the trip in silence. When the taxi pulled along the curb of the Carolina Entertainment building, she opened the door before the car had come to a full stop.

"I'll wait here for you," Connor said.

"No, send the taxi on its way," she countered, thinking of the cost. "If things go well, I'll be at least half an hour. We can have another pick us up when I'm done."

He jerked his chin in agreement and the two of

them exited the taxi. The feel of his palm against the small of her back gave her the assurance she needed as she entered the six-story glass building. She shot a glance in Connor's direction as they crossed the lobby's marble floor. Some sixth sense told her his furrowed brow had little to do with what had happened in the last hour. She shoved the worry to the corner of her thoughts and plastering a smile on her face headed toward the receptionist.

A sudden urge had her doubling back. "Thank you for everything." She gripped his hand. "I couldn't have made the swim or gotten myself here without your help."

He held on when she tried to pull free. "There's something I need to tell you." His lips pressed to a straight line. "I've been trying to find a way to tell you."

"Ms. Madigan?" the receptionist called.

"It'll keep," Avery said, squeezing his hand. "Wish me luck."

"You don't need luck or me."

She took the elevator to the top floor and after being ushered into Preston's posh office by his admin, Avery began the most important sales pitch of her career.

An hour later she was still at it, but that didn't mean things were going well. She was beginning to think the swim ashore had been the easy part of her day. "I can upgrade the meal and beverage service at no additional cost," she said after discussing the regularly scheduled flights and aircraft options.

"You certainly have an answer for everything," Preston responded, his expression impassive.

Avery schooled her own features against the building frustration. Wasn't answering his concerns part of her job? "I assure you, you won't find a company who can offer better service or your entertainers greater luxury," she continued.

He pushed his chair back and rounded his desk. "I don't doubt that, Ms. Madigan."

Sensing he'd heard all he was willing to, she struggled for something to clinch the deal. "Avery," she said, urging him again to use her first name. "As I said before, Flight Innovations is all about service after the sale."

Raising a hand, he cut off the rest of her spiel. "I'm sorry, but I've made my decision. Aviation Options from over in LaGrange was able to give me a better bottom line, and in this economy that means more to me than a posh interior my clients are likely to trash or be too busy to notice."

She let out a breath. The one thing she couldn't offer was a better price. Her boss had taken that out of her hands. "I'm sure there's something we can work out," she countered.

"I'm sorry, but my mind's made up. Thank you for your time." As he shook her hand again, he eyed her dress. "You certainly went above and beyond for your company," he added, referencing the abbreviated explanation she given as to why she arrived in an orange and pink maxi dress.

Preston reached for a jacket hanging from a coat rack by the door. "I'm headed for that wedding I told you about. Why don't I walk you out?"

"Sure," she managed, when all she wanted was to have a moment to collect herself before facing Connor.

Preston chatted as they rode down in the elevator together, telling her about his niece's wedding as if he hadn't just lit a match to the kindling of her career at Flight Innovations.

Walking into the lobby, she blinked to keep the tears that were pooling from making their way down her cheeks. At the sight of Connor waiting for her, her throat tightened. He'd risked so much to get her to this appointment, only to have her fail.

He came to his feet as she drew near. His initial look of concern morphed into a wide-eyed look of panic she couldn't grasp.

"Mr. St. James," Preston said, coming around her to extend his hand. "Did we have an appointment that I've forgotten about?"

"Umm, no," Connor replied, his gaze darting everywhere but at her. "I'm here on another matter."

"Well, that's fine. It'll save me a phone call. Despite Ms. Madigan's best efforts, I'm sending my business your way. You undercut her bid by ten percent."

Whatever Connor said in response was drowned out by her pulse thrumming in her ears. Her mind raced to play catch up to what the two men already knew— Connor's company was Aviation Options.

Avery struggled to breathe past the lump in her throat. "I'll leave you two to celebrate," she managed, stumbling for the door. She raced up the street toward a taxi stand she'd seen coming in. She'd just slipped into the backseat when Connor caught up to her.

He pounded a fist on the window. "Let me explain."

"Drive on," she told the driver. She resisted the

urge to flip Connor off. There wasn't anything he could say that would change the facts. He'd used her to get the details of her company's bid and then lured her onto his boat to make sure she didn't get a chance to deliver it. The pain of that realization sucked the breath out of her.

The betrayal cast her adrift, and she needed to get her arms around her son in the worst possible way. He was the only truly certain thing she had in her life right now. She glanced at the clock on the dashboard ahead. Will and Rob's flight was due in two hours. "Take me to the airport," she said, then leaned her head against the seat and let the tears fall.

God, there really *wasn't* anything he wouldn't do to win.

Chapter Ten

Avery silently urged forward the elderly couple ahead of her in line as they dithered with their collection of oversized suitcases, shopping bags, and carry-ons. A shrill yapping from inside a pet carrier at the lady's feet had her praying its owners weren't on the same Atlanta-bound flight as she. "Here," Avery said, taking hold of one of their enormous suitcases. "Let me help you."

Their half dozen bags stood in contrast to her own empty-handed approach to the next available ticket agent. Too late, she realized she'd neglected to check out of the hotel in her mad dash to escape Connor's betrayal. Unlike the mess she was leaving behind in Wilmington, a quick phone call to the hotel's front desk would take care of her left-behind clothes and laptop. In less than two hours, Will's flight would land, and forty-five minutes later the two of them would be winging their way back home.

Looking over her shoulder one last time, Avery left the ticket counter and joined the queue at the security checkpoint. From the moment she left Connor standing in front of the Carolina Entertainment building, she feared he'd show up wanting a chance to justify his actions. A small part of her wanted him to offer an explanation. On the ride over, she'd come up with a number of questions she'd like to pose to him. Along with a few choice names she wanted to call the lying bastard. The larger part of her simply hoped to slip away to lick her wounds and never lay eyes on him again.

After clearing security, she dropped into a seat at the gate where Rob and Will's flight would soon arrive. Pulling her phone from her pocket, she stared at the darkened screen and wished she could postpone making the dreaded call to her boss. Putting off the inevitable wouldn't make the conversation any easier.

The phone rang once. "Did you get Preston to sign?" he asked in his usual abrupt manner.

Man, the guy really needed to work on his people skills. She visualized him sitting behind his oversized mahogany desk. It didn't take much imagination to conjure up his arrogant sneer.

She wavered on the approach to best break the news to him—the slow build up or cut to the chase. Holding out a sliver of hope that she'd be able to salvage her job, she prayed he'd hear her out. "Mr. Preston liked the amenities we offered, and our aircraft availability impressed him, but the bottom line was more important to him." She drew in a breath. "He's decided on"—her lying lover—"Aviation Options."

Heavy silence filled the air between them. "I see."

But did he? She wondered if he'd given any consideration to the fact the final cost of her proposal was the one thing he'd kept under his control. As much as she wanted to lay all the blame on that one aspect of the deal, the real fault still rested with her.

In the taxi's backseat, she'd replayed the past few days. If she hadn't been so blinded by lust, she'd have seen through Connor's charade—especially when she'd walked into her hotel room to find him in close proximity to her laptop. Why hadn't she thought about the possibility they'd both go into the same field after leaving active duty? Hadn't their history of competition been enough of a warning? It seemed as if they were destined to be pitted against each other during each stage of their lives. Grinding her teeth, she listened as Douglas droned on.

"When the upper management questioned why I was allowing you to pursue this type of new business, I advocated for you. I took a chance that you could pull off this hair-brained idea, and you let me down."

Damn, when she'd left her laptop open on the table, she'd practically handed Connor her pitch. Armed with that knowledge, it would have been no trick for him to call Mr. Preston and ensure his deal was better. Then as added insurance, he'd lured her on his boat where he could keep her from making her appointment.

Having enough of the bashing and bullshit, Avery cut off her boss' tirade. "I did everything humanly possible to win the business." Perhaps not everything. There were some lengths she wasn't willing to go to come out ahead. Unlike others.

"I'm very disappointed in you, Avery. And more than a little surprised."

His lie shouldn't have caused the lancing pain in her chest. He'd set her up for failure since day one. "I'll get the next one, Douglas. I'm scheduled to see the people at Louisiana Gas and Oil on Wednesday. Their contract will bring in nearly as much revenue as Carolina Entertainment's," she said, clinging to some hope that she'd be there to pitch it.

"Here's the thing. I'm not sure passenger transport is the right thing for us. I've been advocating your proposals to the boys upstairs, but you're a hard sell when you can't close the deals. I'm afraid you no longer have a future here. I'm letting you go."

Avery wouldn't beg. As much as she needed the job, she knew a lost cause when it yammered at her over the phone. "I understand," she managed, her voice quivering. She rubbed her sternum against the riot of emotions that had her heart thundering in her chest. First Connor's betrayal and now the loss of her job. "I'll come by next week to collect my things."

"They'll be at the front desk. Please turn in your badge and laptop at that time."

"Got it." Hanging up the phone, she let out a breath. At least the worst was behind her.

****

An hour later, Avery paced in front of Rob and Will's arrival gate. Once she had her arms around her son, she'd figure out how to fix the rest of the disaster that was her life. Her pulse rose as the steady stream of people dwindled to a trickle. She fumbled for her phone, checking the itinerary Rob sent her when they'd made the arrangements for the visitation. She had the right time and the right gate, so where was he? When she saw the crew get off the plane, she couldn't wait a second longer.

Approaching a flight attendant, she asked, "Are there any passengers left on the plane? I'm looking for my son and his father who were supposed to be on this flight."

"No," the woman said. "The plane's empty."

Avery ground her molars. *Dammit.* Rob had missed

the flight. Calling up his number from her list of contacts, she stabbed the screen with more force than necessary. After six rings, the call switched over to voicemail.

"I'm sitting at the gate wondering what the hell's happening, Rob," she said after listening to his prerecorded greeting. "I don't need to remind you Will and I have a flight to Atlanta to catch." Remembering the innumerable times her ex had failed to stick to a plan, she added, "Or perhaps I do." Frustration churned in her stomach, but giving Rob the tongue-lashing he deserved was a waste of her energy. "Call me ASAP and let me know what flight you're on."

Searching for some positive aspect of Rob's perpetual tardiness, she realized at least now she'd have time to return to the hotel for her things. She headed back through the airport concourse toward the front, making a detour at the gate agent's kiosk to change her and Will's flight to the last one out that night. Surely, by then Rob would have managed to get their son back to her.

Just as she was leaving the airline's service desk, someone tapped her on the shoulder. "Ms. Madigan?"

"Yes," she said, hoping it was someone giving her some information about what flight Will was on. Instead a thirty-something guy dressed in a bad suit thrust an envelope at her.

"You've been served, ma'am. Have a nice day."

Served? Blood rang in her ears as she stumbled to a nearby bench. With shaking hands, she opened the envelope and removed the sheets of paper. She skimmed over the petition filed in Polk County Family Court. When she reached the end of the three-page document, she started over again, her mind unwilling to believe the words. Bile burned the back of her throat as she reread the document. Rob was filing for sole custody of Will—in the county where the Gaffney family had reigned for generations.

Avery took a couple steps toward a trashcan in case she became as sick as she felt. This couldn't be happening to her. How had she managed to completely lose her grip on life? She clenched her fist wanting to punch something—anything to vent her impotent rage. Thankfully, good sense prevailed. But then so did the tidal wave of pain. It stole her breath and for the space of a heartbeat, she wanted to reach out to Connor. *How pathetic was that?* No, instead she'd call Steph and Opie. They'd be able to talk her out of doing anything rash, things that might make her predicament worse or land her in jail. Still leaning over the trashcan like a coed on a bender, she drew in steadying breaths.

Avery jerked when her phone came alive in her hand. The sight of her son's face on the screen choked her with emotion. She touched the green button with a finger that trembled. "Will, where are you, baby?"

"Mom." He groaned at her use of the endearment.

"Will, please." She dabbed at tears that spilled down her cheeks. "I need to know where you are." Her voice cracked as fear gripped her throat.

"Are you okay, Mommy? You don't sound like yourself," he said.

"I'm fine," she said, struggling to gain control over her emotions. "You and your father were supposed to be on a flight this evening. I'm just wondering where you are." What if Rob had taken their son out of the country?

"I know," he said. "I told Dad you'd be worried, but he and Tiffany wanted to stay here in Florida a little longer."

Now that she knew Will hadn't been stolen away from her, her temper rose. "Put your dad on the phone."

Some minutes later she ended what she hoped was the last god-awful phone conversation she had to have for a long while. According to Rob, now that he and Tiffany were married, they could provide a more stable home life for Will than she could as a single mom. While he'd been prattling on about their son needing a masculine influence, she'd been figuring out how to keep him from learning she was now an unemployed, single mom. That meant finding a job—any job—as soon as possible. Despite the churning in her stomach, she'd kept her emotions in check as she reminded him in no uncertain terms that until the courts stated otherwise, she had legal custody of their son.

"I'll meet you at the McDonalds on exit 274. Call me if you're running late." Despite the façade she presented, in truth Rob held all the aces. With Will in Florida, and his grandparents—Rob's mother and father—owning half the land in Polk County, she was at his mercy and had only his word that he'd drive their son back to Atlanta in time for school on Monday. She sank to a nearby bench, needing to collect her thoughts. Her sanity hung by the thinnest of wires. One tug and she'd snap.

****

Connor stormed through the airport's front doors, scanning the crowds for Avery. From several yards away, her auburn hair caught his attention. *Finally*. He'd wasted so much time looking at the hotel and feared he'd lost her. Even as he closed the distance, he knew she'd slipped from his grasp as surely as if her flight home had already left.

Even if he never convinced her he hadn't cheated her out of the contract, he couldn't let her leave believing everything about this week had been a lie. Maybe she'd give him a chance to explain. Grasping at the sliver of hope, he headed over to her. His steps slowed as he found her staring at several sheets of paper as if the words proclaimed a death. The touch of his hand to her shoulder had her head jerking up. A mixture of anger and fear distorted her beautiful features. He'd done this to her.

She launched herself at him. "You bastard." She hissed, fisting the front of his shirt. "If it weren't for you, I'd still have a fighting chance."

Damn, her asshole of a boss *had* fired her. But noting the streaks of mascara marring her cheeks, he knew that wasn't what had put the fear in her eyes. His girl was made out of tougher stuff than that. "What happened?" She released his shirt, her shoulders slumping. Then as she let him lead her back to the bench, his pulse soared to triple digits, and not because he was dying for her touch. Recalling she was scheduled to pick up her son from his father today before heading home to Atlanta, he asked, "Where's Will?"

Avery shook her head, and it was several seconds before she found her voice. "Rob's filed for custody here in North Carolina." She met his gaze with haunted eyes. "Now on top of being unemployed, I might lose my son."

A growl escaped his lips. "The fucker! He can't do

that to you—to your son."

She barked a laugh, the bitterness breaking his heart. "That's rich, considering the shit you've pulled over the past few days."

Avery was right. He wasn't much better than her conniving ex-husband. If only he'd been straight with her when he learned they were competing for the same business. When she stood to leave, he took her by the shoulders. "Hold up." He had to offer something to atone for what he'd done. A lie of omission was still a lie. "Let me help."

She pushed him away. "Go away, Titan. I think you've done enough for one day."

He blocked her escape route. "Hit me," he said, jutting out his chin. He clenched his jaw, bracing for the blow he so richly deserved.

She chuffed and rolled her eyes. "Oh, that's just what I need, assault charges on top of everything else."

"Then swear at me," he said, taking her again by the shoulders. "Verbally rip me to shreds. I deserve it, and it'll make you feel better."

As she let out a breath, it seemed all her fight left along with the spent oxygen. She didn't even resist when her steered her back to her seat. "As much as I'd like to lay all the blame for what's happened at your doorstep, you had nothing to do with Rob's actions."

Her absolution did nothing to assuage the guilt knotting his stomach. "Let me see the petition." She thrust the papers toward him and after he read through the legalese, he had to wonder how her ex-husband could sleep at night. Not only was the guy asking for full custody, he wanted child support as well. Connor gave voice to the spark of light in this dark insanity.

"No judge in his right mind would take a six-year-old from his mother," he said, although that wouldn't spare her the pain of a lengthy custody battle. He knew all too well the Gaffney clan's affinity for litigation, having experienced it himself when he first took over the business from Stephen.

Her lips formed a thin line as she nodded. "That thought is the only thing keeping me sane right now." Her gaze met his. Fear dilated her pupils to the point where only a thin halo of gray showed. "But I still have to fight him in court and now without a job, I won't have the money to do it." Accusation laced every word.

Though he'd won Carolina Entertainment's business fairly, she didn't know that. Perhaps in the future he'd get his chance to explain, but for now it fell to him to make this burden lighter for her. "I have an idea that might help, but it won't be easy and you probably won't like it."

She rolled her eyes as she thumbed away a few tears. "At this point, I'll listen to anything you've got."

He leaned closer. "Come work for me." When her eyes widened, he kept talking. "Hear me out." At least she didn't deck him.

Chapter Eleven

Perspiration misted Avery's skin as she hefted the first box off the moving van. By the time she'd climbed two flights of stairs, sweat was trickling down her neck. And back. And between her boobs. She crossed through the propped-open door of her new apartment, set the box in the kitchen, and made a beeline for the back door. She'd meant only to open the glass slider to allow a little breeze to blow through—no sense air-conditioning the place with people in and out. The sight of pine trees moving in the wind caught her attention, and stepping onto the tiny balcony, she fanned the hem of her damp T-shirt to catch the air.

The second-story unit she rented wasn't anything to get excited about, and outside the stand of pines, there wasn't much of a view. Her first priority, other than finding a place she could afford in this ocean-side community, had been its distance from the beach. The further, the better. Truth be told, she didn't care if she ever laid eyes on the ocean again. Her experience back in April confirmed her status as a land lover.

"Where do you want this?" Opie called as he backed into the living room holding one end of her sofa.

"Over there," she said, pointing to the only wall long enough to accommodate its length. He and Bash lowered the sofa then stepped out of the way so Deacon and Will could place her end tables on either end. Steph and Hank followed with more boxes, rounding out her all-hands-on-deck moving crew. The frenetic pace of directing traffic kept her mind off the reasons behind the relocation. And who she'd face come Tuesday morning.

An hour later, Hank entered carrying the rails of a disassembled bunk bed. "That's the last of it," he said, passing through on his way to Will's room.

With the truck unloaded, she shifted gears to getting her son's room set up so he'd have a night to settle in before he left with Stephanie and Opie in the morning. The three kids usually visited back and forth during the summer, but given her new job and the court case, she felt he'd be happier spending time at his honorary aunt and uncle's house. She stopped Hank on his way out the door. "Do you mind?" she asked, holding up her tool kit. "I need an extra pair of hands getting that thing put together."

"Sure," he answered, wiping sweat from his brow. While he held the corner posts in place, she screwed in the rails and in a few minutes they had the bed reassembled.

After sliding the bottom mattress into place, she repeated what she'd been telling her friends all morning, "Thanks for giving up your Saturday. I'm sure you had better things to do during your Memorial Day weekend." Without their help, she'd have had to hire movers—an expense she could ill afford considering the amount she'd had to shell out in attorney's fees.

He shot her one of his easygoing smiles. "No worries. Besides, we're practically family now."

Avery wasn't the only one who'd come home to

find a spouse who hadn't been faithful. She rolled her eyes at his attempted joke. "I'm not sure our exes marrying each other make us relations, but I appreciate your help all the same." While the two of them finished arranging Will's room, her mind rewound to the events of three years ago. Tiffany and Rob's affair created plenty of gossip for her and Hank to face, along with enough pain to last a lifetime. She wondered how he'd handled the wedding news but couldn't work out how to broach the subject without potentially embarrassing him. As for her, the wedding drama was a drop in her emotional bucket compared to the custody battle she was now fighting. The thoughts of Tiffany raising her son turned her stomach, and she quickly shoved that image to the dark corner of her imagination. There'd be plenty time to ponder that nightmare in the period leading up to their first court date, just a few weeks away. Thanks to the Gaffney's influence in the county, the custody case had been fast-tracked to the front of the court docket.

As she and Hank put the wrench and hammer back in her toolkit, Will careened into the room. "Can I go to the pool? It's only a couple buildings over."

"Maybe later," she said, looking around the box-filled room. "I can't stop what I'm doing to go with you now." After she got his room squared away, she still needed to tackle the kitchen and bathroom.

"Mom! I'm not a baby," he huffed. "I can go by myself."

She'd made a point of ensuring not to pass on her issues with water and had enrolled him in Aqua Tots before his first birthday. She still wasn't willing to let her six-year-old swim without supervision even with a lifeguard. "You might not be a baby, but you're still not old enough to go on your on."

"But…" he countered.

Her head warred with her heart. They had so many difficult moments in the past several weeks that she hated adding to the list. Though she emphasized the benefits of being closer to his father and extended family, leaving neighbors and friends had been a series of gut-wrenching good-byes. She thumbed over her shoulder at the now reconstructed bed. "Get your toys and books unpacked, and I'll see if one of the guys will take you."

His shoulder dropped. "Okay."

Skirmish averted, she ruffled his hair on her way out. "I'll be back to check on your progress in a while." Once they were out of earshot, she turned to Hank, who'd played witness to the parent-child battle of wills. "Sorry about that. He's usually not that argumentative."

He looked over his shoulder and shrugged. "I don't have any experience with kids, but it seems like you're doing a good job to me."

"I'm trying," she said, heading toward the kitchen to tackle the dozen boxes waiting for her there. She stepped into the narrow room to find Stephanie arranging glasses in the cabinet.

"I thought it made sense to put the glasses next to the refrigerator," she said. "I hope you don't mind that I'm taking over."

"Not at all." She shot her best friend a grateful smile for checking off one more item on her to-do list. "I don't know what I'd do without you and Opie."

Stephanie shook her head and smiled. "That's what friends do. I'm just sorry you're going through so much all at once."

"Me too," Avery said with a bitter chuckle. It had been an up-and-down couple of months, and she was ready to get off the drama coaster.

"Men are such jerks," Steph added with a laugh as she reached for a stack of plates.

"Hey," Opie said, entering in the room. "I resent being lumped into the same group as those two dumbasses you're no doubt referring to." He wrapped his arms around his wife's waist. "I'm completely housebroken, I'll have you know."

"Okay," she conceded. "Not all men are jerks."

No. Just the ones she fell in love with. Avery shook herself loose from the urge to wallow in self-pity. "How about I order lunch?"

Thirty minutes later when the pizzas arrived, she went in to check on Will's progress. "You hungry?"

"You bet."

When wasn't he? Her boy was growing up before her eyes. She took in his attempts at making his bed and the boxes he'd emptied. "Wow, you've really done a great job."

"Thanks," he said, beaming. "Does that mean I can go swimming?"

"Absolutely. I already talked to Hank, and he said he'd be glad to take you." She turned away.

"Mom, wait. Can I have the little TV in here?" He pointed to the corner of the room where he'd arranged his Lego table and beanbag chair. "I wanted to make a place to relax. You know—a man cave."

Avery suppressed the smile, seeing the intent look on the little guy's face. She shook her head. "You know the rule, and I already made a concession for the tablet your dad bought. I don't want you holed up in here all the time." Their time together was too precious to spend in different rooms engaged in separate activities.

"Dad lets me at his place," he shot back.

The verbal dart hit its mark even if it was one she dodged every time he returned from visiting his dad. Just once she wanted to play the good cop. "It's not up for discussion. Now come eat some lunch so you and Hank can have plenty of time at the pool."

Hours later when all the furniture was in its place, the kitchen squared away, and Will tucked in bed, Avery stood at the door saying good-bye to the last of her helpers. Stephanie lingered repeating another generous offer. "We can stay longer if you need us to."

"No. I can handle the rest."

"Are you sure there's nothing else we can do for you?"

"Yeah," Opie interjected. "If you've got any exes that need killing, I can take care of that while I'm in the area. I come cheap and bury them deep."

Steph elbowed him in the ribs. "David, stop. You're not helping."

Emotion clogged her throat despite his joke. After accepting Connor's job offer, these two had been her first call. Opie had made his outrageous offer for the first time then. She declined, of course, but not before entertaining a little fantasy that included mishaps befalling both men. Then her former wingman got serious and offered to dip into his retirement savings to help with her upcoming legal expenses. "I've got it but thanks. I'll have Will ready at eight o'clock in the morning."

Avery closed the door on her two friends and

turned to tackle the cardboard soldiers lining the dining room walls. Sometime after eleven, she emptied the last box of the night. The rest could wait. Having sent Will off to bed several hours before, she wandered into the kitchen for a snack to find Steph had left a bottle of her favorite red wine on the counter along with an overly large glass. In a pair of seconds she'd located the corkscrew and poured herself a generous amount. Despite her still lengthy to-do list, the sofa called to her. She collapsed on it, propping her feet on the coffee table.

Just as she was taking a sip, Will slipped into the room. "Mommy, I've been thinking."

She patted the cushion next to her. "About what?" she asked, reining in the urge to draw him in next to her. In the past few months he'd been resistant to letting her hug him as much as he used to.

"I don't want to go with Uncle David and Aunt Stephanie tomorrow."

"What?" Her maternal alarm screamed. "Why? You were looking forward to it earlier."

He shrugged. "I changed my mind."

"Talk to me. Is it the move? I'm sure once you get back, there'll still be plenty of time to make new friends before school starts."

He nodded but didn't say anything. Her mind raced with worry, but she held back from peppering him with questions. He'd get there when he was ready. "You'll be lonely when I leave."

His tender words struck her like a blow. She'd tried so hard to shield him from his father's legal machinations and the hurt she'd been nursing from Connor's betrayal. She gave into the mothering impulse and caught him up in a fierce hug. "I'll be fine," she said after a moment. "I'll miss you like crazy, but I'll have plenty to keep me busy while you're gone."

"You seem so sad lately," he whispered.

"I'm fine," she repeated. Perhaps if she said the mantra enough, she'd come to believe it. "I'm just overtired." She kissed the top of his head, remembering when he smelled of baby shampoo. "Besides it's not your job to look after me." Tamping down on her emotions, she put an end to the debate. "Back to bed. We've got an early start in the morning." She kissed his cheek then released him.

After tucking him in, exhaustion covered her like the humidity outside. She gave serious consideration to collapsing on the sofa to sleep rather than making the few steps to her bed. She grabbed a throw blanket and curled up on the sofa, but even as she closed her eyes, she couldn't find any rest. Instead her mind churned over the past several weeks, focusing in on the deepest hurt. She'd been such a fool for believing Connor cared for her. His job offer—though appreciated—was simply a way to assuage his guilt. Now she'd have to look into his handsome face and pretend *nothing* he'd done to her mattered.

****

Tuesday morning Connor placed an oversized coffee cup on Hillary's desk. "Two sweeteners and lots of cream," he announced to his admin. At least a couple times a week he stopped to buy her coffee on his way in, especially if they had an early morning. Today called for something more than gas station java.

Without looking away from her computer screen, the petite brunette's manicured hand zeroed in on the cup. "Where'd you get this?" she asked after the first sip. In addition to being Jill-of-all-trades at work, and stray dog rescuer at home, the single mom in her mid-fifties was a self-proclaimed caffeine fiend. She practically mainlined the stuff and usually wasn't picky about her sources. "It's like nectar of the gods."

"The same place I got these," he said, opening the lid and placing the pink box within reach. "I've got Sofia bringing in the other boxes for the crew." Standing in line at Daylight Bakery, he couldn't decide if he was getting the three dozen doughnuts to celebrate finalizing the Carolina Entertainment contract or to medicate her before announcing he'd hired Avery. Although he'd made the offer to her back in April, he hadn't wanted to tell his admin about his new hire until the details of the account were finalized

Hillary's eyes lit up. "You got the details worked out."

"Yep, I got ink on paper." His victory fell short of complete considering its unintended consequences to Avery's life. All the same, he mustered some enthusiasm for his hardworking admin's benefit. She'd stuck by him during the god-awful early days when others would have looked for employment elsewhere. "Our first gig will be flying a band on their tour of the Southeast."

"Fantastic," she said, wiping frosting from the corner of her mouth with her finger and then licking it off. "As soon as I grab the files I need, I'll be in your office so we can map out the week." She grinned as she reached for another doughnut. "Paying bills is so much more fun when there's money in the account."

"Don't rush. I need a minute to check my emails."

He also still had to find a smooth way of breaking his other news. While the new business would go a long way toward stabilizing his company, it would be at least a while before they saw actual revenue. The next month or so would be tricky, and that was before factoring in the added stress of Avery's presence. He'd have to work on his poker face to keep everyone from figuring out there was more to their relationship than being old navy buddies.

After flipping on the overhead lights he rounded his desk and powered up his dinosaur of a computer. Top on his to-buy list once the finances evened out was new office equipment. After the half century it took for the machine to boot up, he opened his email, scanning down his inbox half expecting to see one from Avery announcing she'd changed her mind. There wasn't— which filled him with equal parts anticipation and dread.

He'd combed through a tenth of the emails sitting in his inbox when the door to his office opened. "I've got Sofia started on her to-do list this morning," Hillary said, balancing an armload of manila files along with two crullers and her coffee.

"Did she give you any grief?" While his niece could be helpful when the mood struck her, it usually did so when she planned to ask for a favor later. Going by the rocky start they'd had already this morning, clearly she wouldn't be hitting him up for more pocket money any time soon.

"No, she was fine," Hillary said, setting the files and her coffee on his desk.

He gave her a moment to settle in. They'd worked out the ritual over the past few years, meeting in his office to get ahead of any issues that might be facing them during the week. After arranging the files across the nearly bare surface of his desk, she pulled forward one of the club chairs he kept for visitors.

He raked his hands through his hair then dove in at the deep end. "I hired someone to manage our clients and take over new sales. She starts in an hour."

Hillary froze halfway into the chair. "You did what?" Her backside plopped into the seat.

"Last month I ran into someone I used to fly with in the navy." In response to her still stunned expression, he elaborated. "Actually, she and I were competing for the Carolina Entertainment account. Mad Dog gave me a real run for my money, and I'm sure she'll work just as hard for us. There isn't a non-compete clause so she can keep pursuing any leads she was working on at her old job." When Hillary arched an eyebrow, he realized he was yammering and clamped his lips together.

"She's commission only, right?"

"Base salary, plus ten percent." In bringing Avery on board, he'd blown Hillary's carefully constructed budget. But hiring her was the right thing to do. When she opened her mouth, he cut her off. "I know what I'm doing. Give Mad two months, and she'll be earning her keep and then some."

A pair of heartbeats passed in silence before she spoke. "And in the meantime?"

He let out a breath. "That's what we're about to figure out," he said, giving his admin credit for not quitting on the spot.

An hour later, they'd squeezed every penny out of the budget until Honest Abe was screaming for mercy. He arrowed to the bottom of the spreadsheet. "As long as we don't encounter any unexpected expenses, we should be okay."

"Good Lord willing and the creek don't rise," she echoed with the merest touch of sarcasm. Then she closed her folder and stood. "If that's everything, I'll get started cutting these checks."

"Okay," he said, feeling like shit that he'd made her job more difficult. "Send Mad in when she gets here." He'd no more gotten through the first email when Sofia slipped into the room. She flopped into the chair and let out a sigh. "If Meghan's mom can come get me, can I go to her house for a while?"

After she'd already spent Memorial Day weekend at her best friend's house, he hesitated to say "yes." It wasn't Mrs. Barnes's job to babysit Sofia. "Maybe later."

"I'm bored." She groaned like it was fatal.

"I'll take you girls to the mall tonight. Right now, I've got a new employee coming in this morning, and I need to prepare a few things. Go see if Hillary has anything else for you to do?"

"Let me hang out in here, please," she said, sitting up. "She'll just send me off to clean something. That's what she always does when she runs out of office work."

Connor swallowed his frustration. "Okay, but could you please for the time being, act like you don't hate me?" They had a particularly contentious argument over curfew the previous night, the likes of which could easily trump some Civil War battles fought nearby.

Sofia smirked. "I don't hate you, Uncle Connor. It's just a phase I'm going through. I'm supposed to act like this."

He rolled his eyes. God, just when he thought she'd drive him over the edge, she made him see the lighter side of life. Something he would need if he was to survive seeing Avery every day.

****

Avery killed the engine of her car and drew in a steadying breath. The first day on a new job was never easy, but this had to take the blue ribbon for most difficult. She flipped down the visor mirror, smoothing her hand over her chignon. Since April she'd nurtured her anger toward Connor, all the better to use it as a shield. Below the protective barrier, her heart still ached with his betrayal nearly as strongly as did the knowledge he was all that stood between her and losing custody of Will. He didn't need to know that. In fact, she vowed to never reveal how much she still hurt.

Looking away from her appearance, she scanned her new work environment. The hangar that housed Aviation Options was like everything else in LaGrange: smaller, older, and less brash than Atlanta. Under different circumstances she might have enjoyed her new life in coastal North Carolina. An ex-husband who wanted to take their child away from her and a former lover who was the key to making sure that didn't happen cast a cloud over any enjoyment she might feel.

"Quit stalling," she said, reaching for the car door handle.

She crossed the parking lot, noting it could use a topcoat of asphalt and the hangar itself was a little weather worn. At the threshold of the open bay, she caught a glimpse of how much Connor had needed to win the contract with Carolina Entertainment. Though the place was squared away, the tug trucks and auxiliary power units were decades old, their blue and white paint faded with age. The contrast lay with the gleaming aircrafts parked inside. The high-end twin-engine planes dominated the hanger like royal princes among paupers.

Seeing a small door at the far end, she headed in that direction. As Avery stepped inside the office area, a middle-aged woman rose to meet her. "You must be Commander Madigan," she said, extending her hand. "I've heard a lot about you." Along with the firm handshake came a top-to-bottom assessment. "I'm Hillary Cook, Titan's admin. He wanted to see you first thing. His office is right this way."

"Thanks," Avery said, her pulse kicking up a notch. Trailing behind the woman, she noted the well-worn theme followed that of the hangar. The monitor sitting atop Hillary's metal desk looked like a throwback to the nineties. She rapped on the open door but took only that first step inside, blocking Avery's view. Anxiety prickled along her scalp as she awaited that first look.

"I brought her in like you asked," Hillary announced. "When you're done with her, I need her to fill out some employment papers." She then stepped out of the way.

Seeing him, Avery's breath caught. Seated behind an oversized mahogany desk, the wall behind him covered in photographic evidence of his military glory, he gave the outward appearance of the business mogul. A titan. A pristine-white dress shirt—sleeves rolled to the elbow—and gray tie completed the look. But his tousled hair hinted at his barely restrained energy.

"Sure thing, Hill," he said. Taking to his feet, he

crossed to the front of his desk as she stepped fully inside the room. His goatee-bracketed mouth turned up in a smile, but the spark she'd seen so many times during their time together was absent from his eyes. Perhaps the past several weeks had taken their toll on him as well. That didn't stop him from looking like the devil himself. Or her body's reaction to him. Her mouth went dry, and her brain went completely offline.

"Welcome aboard," he said taking another step closer but not offering his hand as his admin had. He shifted his weight from foot to foot. "Have you found a new place? If you haven't, I can help you look."

"I did, thank you."

"No problems getting Will settled?"

"None," she said. "He's with Steph and Opie. I thought…" She let the rest of her explanation die.

Connor quirked an eyebrow as if he wanted her to finish her thought.

She shook her head, ruthlessly stomping the urge to share. They weren't lovers or friends either, so he didn't need to know she managed to convince Rob that spending the summer with Opie and Stephanie was the best thing for Will right now. If her ex-husband was intent on dragging her through the courts, the least she could do was keep their son from playing witness to the mess.

The half-smile faded altogether, and he let out a breath. "This is my niece, Sofia," he said, pointing to the teen sitting legs folded in a side chair. "She's helping Hillary out in the office during her summer vacation." He patted the girl's blonde hair. "Say hi to Avery."

"Hi to Avery," Sofia parroted with a wave.

Her attention shifted to the girl. Testament to how much his presence captured her full attention was the fact there'd been another person in the room during their conversation. Avery's gaze darted between Sofia and Connor. They had the same strong jaw and piercing blue eyes, although his were a bit shrewder than his niece's and sitting below knitted brows.

"Would you rather everyone called you Mad?" he asked.

"Either is fine," she said. The days they'd spent as lovers she'd grown to like the name she'd been born with. Especially when uttered by Connor as he made love to her. Her throat tightened just thinking about it. In the past few weeks, her emotions toward Connor swung between gratitude that he'd offered her a lifeline and anger at his lies. Then throw in the fact she was still in love with him, and she was pretty much one wrong move away from a full-blown mascara-ruining meltdown. She shoved those emotions into a far corner of her mind *and* locked the door. Letting them run the show had gotten her in this predicament in the first place. "What's my first assignment?" she asked.

Later that morning, Avery adjusted the phone she'd wedged between her ear and shoulder. "You're on the books for June sixth through August ninth, Mr. Preston." She jotted down details on her notepad. Anxious to distract herself from the ache of seeing Connor again, she tackled the job of proving his decision to hire her was more than a good way to assuage his guilt. "We'll have a plane waiting for your people at zero-six hundred."

Carolina Entertainment's vice president reiterated his pleasure at learning the news of her job change.

"I'm happy to be working for Mr. St. James as well," she responded with a lie that fell well into gray territory. Besides having to daily face the man who betrayed her, the pointed stares Connor's admin kept shooting her made it clear not to expect a warm welcome from her fellow employee. "I'm sure you'll be happy with the service you receive from us," she said before hanging up.

After ending the call, she kept her attention trained on the notepad where she'd jotted down the pertinent information on the charter flight which would transport an indie rock band on its tour of the south. Either Hillary would decide to give her a chance, or she wouldn't. Regardless, Avery was determined to give Connor her best.

Avery thumbed through her list of prospects, her thoughts drifted to the other issue weighing heavily on her heart. Saying good-bye to Will never got easier no matter how many times she did it or how well cared for he'd be. Stephanie called late last night to say she'd gotten him settled in for the night with a minimum of fuss. While her best friend's assurance eased some of Avery's worry, it didn't alleviate the ache in her chest. She desperately hoped Rob didn't win his petition for full custody, making the separation a permanent one.

She redoubled her efforts to immerse herself in her new job. Until the first hearing scheduled in a few weeks, there was nothing to do but wait and wonder what prompted Rob to suddenly act like the involved parent.

As Avery penned a list of new business prospects, Hillary's creaking chair drew her attention. The woman pushed back from her seat, crossing the space separating their two desks. "We need to talk."

Avery blinked in surprise. "Sure," she said after a moment. "What's up?"

"Grab your purse. I'm treating you to lunch."

Impressed with the other woman's straight-shooting approach but also still expecting a come-to-Jesus conversation, she complied with the directive. At least they'd get Hillary's objections out in the open where they could deal with them. The two women left through the hangar door, then crossed the parking lot to Hillary's car.

"Downtown doesn't have a lot to offer, but there's a place on the square that serves more than hamburgers and fries."

"Sounds great," Avery said, slipping into the passenger seat.

They made the short trip into town. Not much had changed since the last time she'd traveled to the coastal North Carolina hamlet for one of the Gaffney clan's family reunions. She tried not to blame the town for the chilly reception she received each time she came to LaGrange. His family never thought much of either her or her military ambitions, preferring their women as sweet and docile as their iced tea. After a few miles they pulled in front of a familiar restaurant that did have a great upscale menu. "Oh, Le Peep is still open."

In response to Hillary's arched eyebrow, she explained. "My ex-husband grew up here."

As they trailed behind the hostess to their booth, she asked. "Who's your ex? My family's lived here since the mid-1800s, so I'm probably related to him."

Great, my day just keeps getting better. Even if Hillary didn't belong to some branch of the Gaffney family tree, the prolific clan held great sway in this section of North Carolina. If she was fond of them, she might count it as another strike against Avery that she'd divorced the crown prince of Polk County. "Robert Gaffney," she said. "He's Marjory and Dilbert's son."

"Definitely *not* related," Hillary answered, her expression twisted like she'd smelled something bad. "But my youngest sister went out with Robbie in high school."

Avery chuckled. When they'd been married, he insisted everyone call him 'Rob' or 'Robert.'

"Let's hope he was more faithful to her than he was to me."

Hillary looked over the top of her menu, her eyes wide with curiosity. "I get the feeling there's quite a story there."

She waved away the prompt to share. "Forget I said that. It's in the past."

With a shrug, Hillary went back to scanning the menu. Their waitress came along soon after, taking their order and cutting some of the awkward silence. She'd cleared one hurdle but still had to convince Titan's admin she'd be worth her salary. When the late-teens waitress returned with their drink orders, Avery used her straw to stir her diet cola and searched for a way to broach the unspoken reason behind the lunch invitation. As she discarded one segue after another, their salads arrived.

"I'll come straight out and ask this because Titan certainly won't give me the straight poop," Hillary said, firing off the opening shot. "Why did he give you this job?"

Avery drew in a breath and lowered her fork. A

direct question deserved a direct answer. "When Connor beat me out of the Carolina Entertainment business, my boss fired me."

The woman clucked sympathetically, prompting another round of honesty.

"That same day I found out Rob's petitioning for full custody of our son. I guess Connor felt guilty about me losing my job and threw me a lifeline so I'd have the money for an attorney."

Hillary's expression softened. "That's just like Titan. When he took over after his brother committed suicide, he paid me out of his own pocket rather than laying me off."

Avery's eyes widened as she processed the news Stephen's death came at his own hands. Though she sympathized with the deep grief his brother's death must have caused Connor, she fought the urge to see him in the same glowing light as the other woman did. So what if he had a soft spot for women in tough situations. His actions helped to put her in the tailspin. She also didn't like being anyone's charity case. "I'm grateful to him for the job, but know this—I'll earn back my salary in new business."

"I'm sure you will, but I think this is also one of those cases where there's more to the story than what you're telling." She fixed Avery with another pointed look. "But that can wait until some other day," she said before taking a bite of her food.

Avery's shoulders relaxed. At least she wouldn't be battling wars on two fronts. She took a deep breath, for the first time looking around the small restaurant decorated with lace curtains and hanging ferns. By the front door, a poster taped to the window caught her eye.

She dropped her fork. How had she missed Rob's deceptively sincere smile staring at her? *Elect Robert Gaffney for Congress.*

Hillary followed her gaze. "It looks like Robbie's trying to mend his bad-boy ways. He's running against Harrison Wheeler in the primary coming up in July."

So that's why he's suddenly playing the involved father role! Even as the missing pieces slid together, her stomach twisted at the realization Rob was using their son to perfect his image as the ideal candidate. "When did this happen?"

"About four months ago," Hillary answered. "You didn't know?"

She shook her head. "He never expressed an interest in politics when we were married."

"It didn't mesh with the Robbie I knew either, but from what I've read in *The LaGrange Ledger*, he's giving Congressman Wheeler a run for his money. He's spent over a hundred thousand dollars so far in his campaign."

Avery picked at her salad. No telling how much he'd be spending in legal fees in order to solidify his image as the perfect family man. While she'd been grateful to Connor for the job before learning Rob's motivation for seeking custody of Will, now she was doubly so. It even looked like she'd won over his admin.

"Don't worry too much, sweetie," Hillary said, patting her hand. "The people around here might be a little backward, but we're not idiots. It'll all come out in the wash."

"God, I hope so." She suddenly felt like she'd eaten rock instead of lettuce. She'd battled for what she'd wanted her whole life—fought against her father's expectations for her career and her superior officers' gender bias. This time, she had more to lose than her career.

Chapter Twelve

Connor shifted in his chair, trying to find a comfortable position. When that didn't work, he adjusted the crick in his neck. Two weeks as Avery's boss and his whole body ached from stress. It wasn't only the effort of reining in his feelings for her that took a toll on his nerves. Looking into her beautiful face and knowing how much she loathed him—both for the mistaken belief he'd betrayed her and for being dependent on him—kept him up at night.

"It looks like I've covered all the bases with Carolina Entertainment, and Growers' Co-op should be ready to sign as soon as I get the final numbers over to them." Tension played across her face, along with the dark circles under her eyes that revealed her weariness. She hid it behind positive, upbeat dialogue. "And I've got a meeting with Louisiana Gas and Oil next week."

He diverted his personal musings long enough to run the numbers on the income her new business was generating. "Excellent," he said. "If you worked this much magic at Flight Innovations, I'm surprised they were willing to let you go."

"If you're happy, I'm happy," she said, her voice perfectly level. Only the creases at the corners of her eyes betrayed her emotions. "If that's all you need, I'll get back to my desk." She closed her tablet and stood.

"Got any plans for the weekend?" he asked,

desperate to do something to ease some of the tension arcing between them and give him a running start on the explanation he'd been churning over in his mind. His attempt at small talk fell flat as she narrowed her eyes at him.

"Nothing in particular," she said, then turned away.

He wanted to leap across the desk and block her from leaving. "Hold up, Mad."

She froze, her back still to him. It was time to set the record straight. He couldn't stand another moment of her thinking he cheated her out of the contract. The words poised on his lips—the facts, his fears—he'd cop to it all. Her rigid spine and the weariness he'd seen on her face stopped him from leaping to his own defense.

"How are you doing?"

Her shoulders moved as she breathed, but by the time she faced him she'd wrestled into submission whatever emotion that had been bubbling inside her. Her features were as beautifully smooth as Venus de Milo and just as cold. "I'm fine."

"You all unpacked at your new place?"

"Almost."

Keep her talking. "That's good. And Will? Have you heard from him?"

She crossed her arms over her body. "I have."

He walked around the front of his desk, sitting on the edge. "I meant what I said. If you need time off to meet with your attorney or anything else, it's yours."

"I won't," she bit out. Then she met his gaze. "Thank you anyway."

He blew out a breath. "Listen, I think it would be a good idea if we finally address the elephant in the room." He took her silence for assent and plunged

147

ahead. "I want you to know how sorry I am for how things ended between us. I never meant to hurt you."

She turned her face, staring out the window. His hands ached to cup her cheek and look into her eyes. To feel her impossibly smooth skin. Thanks to his actions, he'd made sure that would never happen again. She'd never let him get that close, much less tolerate his touch. "I pursued you for the reasons I told you—for us to have a few days of fun. I never used what you told me about your pitch to gain the upper hand." He gripped the edge of the desk. "I was tempted to read it off your laptop—real tempted—so that's why I suggested we take out my boat. Not because I wanted to keep you from your appointment."

She looked up. Pain turned her gray eyes the color of the sea after a storm. "I just have one question."

Do I love you? Hell, yes!

"Why didn't you just tell me we were competing for the same business?" Anger flashed in her eyes. "It's not like we haven't been down this road a hundred times before."

He asked himself the same question and each time come to the same conclusion. Fear and greed: and not fear of the company folding or greed for money. It was for her, and she deserved to know that. He drew in a breath, hoping his words would make things better between them—not add to the awkwardness. He also vowed from here on he'd be perfectly honest with her no matter the result. "I was falling for you, Avery, and I didn't want to risk that you wouldn't believe me." He raked his fingers through his hair. God, there wasn't anything he wouldn't give to redo that decision. "I know that doesn't seem right considering how things ended, or mean much after what happened to you. But at the time, it was all that I could think about."

She bit her lip then after a moment she nodded. "You're right. It doesn't change where we are now." Some of the tension eased from her shoulders. She met his gaze. "But it does help to know I wasn't as big of a fool as I thought I'd been."

If loving her made him a fool, he'd don the jester's cap. That much he didn't regret. He couldn't stand her thinking she was anything less than the brilliant, worthy competition she'd always been. "You're nobody's fool. We just have some bad karma. That's all."

"That's true," she said, then smiled just the least little bit. "Thanks for clearing things up. It means a lot." With that she turned her back on him again. This time he let her.

After Avery left, he tried to refocus his thoughts to the mountain of work on his desk. He failed miserably. His efforts to ease the tension between them hadn't been the shining success he'd hoped since it still left him in the predicament of loving a woman he couldn't have. At least it healed some of her hurt, and that was what counted. Maybe with time they'd even be friends. Cold comfort, especially after knowing what it felt like to bask in her love.

Moments later, Sofia sauntered into his office. "What's up, little bit?" he asked, giving up on concentrating on work.

She cocked her head, smiling sweetly. "I'm finished with the filing you asked me to do."

"Excellent," he said. "Did you take those letters to the post office as well?"

"Yes, and I also emptied the waste baskets without

149

even being asked."

His parental antenna went up. Detecting when his niece was up to something might be a new skill, but it was fully functional thanks to intense training during their first year together and his own misspent youth. "That's wonderful."

"Have you noticed how I've been acting more mature? Not at all like a fifteen-year-old."

"I have. Thank you for taking the initiative."

She crossed over to his side of the desk and perched on the edge. "I was wondering if I could go to a birthday party on the twenty-seventh. It's for a friend of mine from school." She looked at him with wide, innocent eyes.

Here it comes. "How old is this friend turning?" he asked, not crazy about her hanging out with some of the older kids at her high school.

"*She's* turning sixteen," she said, tapping into another one of his concerns. His inclination was to give her everything her heart desired. Indulgence wouldn't make up for the things she'd suffered in her short life.

"Where is it, and are how many adults are chaperoning?"

"The party's at Alexia's house in the West Hampton subdivision."

He cocked an eyebrow, not impressed that the girl's family lived in the poshest neighborhood in LaGrange. At one time, the St. James family had been the big fish in their little pond. It hadn't stopped him and Stephen from getting into trouble. Perhaps the social standing and money even made it easier.

She stood, planting her fists on her hips. "Don't you trust me?" she shrilled.

"You, I trust," he answered after taking a deep breath to settle his rising impatience. "It's everyone else who's suspect." Especially boys—they were from the devil. "Let me talk to Alexia's parents, and then I'll think about it."

She stamped her foot. "I'm so tired of you treating me like a baby."

"Take it, or leave it."

Her growl probably could be heard over in the next county. After she stormed out of the room, Connor pinched the bridge of his nose. Two tours in the Gulf and parenting would be the death of him.

****

Avery returned to her desk and went through the motions of opening her laptop. *Connor hadn't cheated.* Grounded in reality, her ego could deal with losing in a fair fight. The newfound truth should have offered a greater measure of relief. Instead, a cocktail of confusion, sadness, and regret swirled inside her. As much as his words soothed her pride, it still left them at an impasse. He hadn't trusted her enough to tell her the truth. His action said as much about her as it did him, and now they were entwined in this boss/employee tango.

At the thunderous crash of a door being slammed, Avery's attention darted down the hall. Sofia stormed past and then plopped into the seat at her small desk in the corner of the open area she shared with the two other women. Avery made eye contact with the other woman, who shook her head and returned to her work. She did the same, studiously training her gaze on the computer screen in front of her.

As Sofia's huffing turned to quiet crying, her heart

went out to the girl—to Connor as well since they were rowing the same single-parent dingy. Weeks ago at the beginning of their relationship, she'd offered her help. With their tense détente, did she dare offer unsolicited advice now? She bit her lip wondering how he'd feel about her reaching out to his niece.

Tucking her purse under her arm, Avery walked over to the girl. "Want to go to lunch?"

Sofia dashed the tears from her cheeks.

"My treat."

Her gaze darted to Connor's office. "Okay, I guess."

Avery called over her shoulder to Hillary. "Sofia and I are going to Le Peeps for lunch. Want to join us?"

Hillary's smile eased her lingering concerns how the gesture might be perceived. "I'll hold down the fort. You two go ahead."

"Can I bring you that Asian chicken salad you liked the last time we were there?"

"Thanks. That would be great. I'll pay you when you get back," the woman called.

The two crossed the hangar in a silence that continued as they settled into Avery's car. The girl's body language and the fact they barely knew each other put asking the reason for the melodrama off the list.

As she racked her brain for a teen-friendly topic of conversation, she also had to block out the ever-increasing number of *Elect Robert Gaffney to Congress* signs dotting the side of the road. By the time they reached downtown, the silence was nearly as oppressive as her ex's face grinning at her. "Are you having a good summer?"

"Not especially." The girl continued staring out the

window. Avery parked the car in front of the restaurant still mentally discarding one topic of conversation after another. Finally, when they were seated inside the cute bistro on the west side of the square, she hit on something that might require more than a two-word answer. "What classes will you be taking when school starts back in the fall?"

Sofia shrugged and continued to stare at the menu. "Nothing exciting. AP Lit, International Studies, Anatomy, and Trig."

Interesting—Connor's niece might be a little on the melodramatic side, but she was a bright drama queen. "Those are some great courses. I don't think I took trig until my senior year."

More crickets chirping and Avery began to think she'd made the wrong call reaching out to the girl. Clearly, she wasn't the kind likely to open up, or even talk much—something she remembered most teenaged girls being pros at.

"I like that outfit your wearing. Is it new?" In the weeks she worked at Aviation Options, she hadn't seen the girl wear the same outfit twice.

A smile played at the corner of Sofia's mouth as she brushed her hand over the skirt. "I bought it last week at Aeropostale."

The skirt was asymmetrical—short in the front and longer in the back—with black and purple chevrons that created an overall edgy, youthful look Avery couldn't pull off. On the fifteen-year-old it worked. "You have a good eye for fashion."

Sofia let out a breath. "Thanks. I also bought a party dress, but I guess I won't have a reason to wear that."

Melissa Klein

Was that an opening or an off-the-cuff statement? "You never know. Maybe a special occasion will come along."

"Not if Uncle Connor has anything to do with it. He won't let me do anything."

"I'm sure he has your best interest at heart," she said, feeling a kinship with Connor since Rob often put her in the position of playing Bad Cop.

Sofia's gaze darted up to hers. "That's what he says. He's just worried that I'll start drinking or doing drugs like my parents did."

Avery's eyes widened at the girl's candor. "Then surely you can understand his fears."

She rolled her eyes. "Yeah, but can't he see, I won't do that because I have seen what it does to a person?"

Wow! Not many adults had that amount of foresight, much less a teen. Avery reached across the table, squeezing her hand. "Just keep doing what you're doing, and he'll eventually come around."

"Not before next Saturday he won't," she said, tossing down her fork and crossing her arms. "There's a party I want to go to, and I bet a million dollars he'll find a way to not let me go." The girl offered up a doe-eyed look. "Unless someone talked him into it."

There was no way in hell she'd take that bait. Instead, Avery countered with, "I tell you what, if he decides not to let you go, I'll help you come up with something else to do." It had been so long since she'd been a teen, she had no clue what that *something* might be. "What if I take you and a couple of your friends for a mani/pedi and a movie?"

Sofia chewed on her bottom lip, before a smile

154

broke out. "You'd do that?"

"Absolutely. As many girls as will fit in my car."

"It wouldn't be as cool as getting to go to Alexia Gaffney's birthday party, but I'll take it."

Despite not knowing the birthday girl, her name rang in Avery's ears. Not everyone in Rob's family was manipulative and underhanded, surely. Besides, as protective as Connor was, no doubt he knew every detail about the girl and her party.

Chapter Thirteen

A few days later, Connor returned to the hangar after dropping Sofia off at Meghan's house. He crossed the parking lot, worry niggling at the back of his mind. Something was up with his niece. Earlier that morning she'd reacted calmly to his veto of the birthday party when days before she'd touted it as the high water mark of her social life. He'd talked with the parents of her friends as well as the birthday girl's rather bemused mother. His decision boiled down to a lack of adult supervision. Sofia accepted his decision with a shrug, saying Avery offered to entertain her and some friends instead. He tried not to borrow trouble. Who could predict the reaction of a teenaged girl? Certainly not him.

As he entered the hangar, his footsteps echoed in the cavernous space. Another benefit of hiring Avery, she'd closed so many deals, Aviation Options' fleet spent very little time idle. A quick maintenance check between flights and they were off on another run. He'd even pressed her into service, having her fly some medical equipment up to Raleigh yesterday. He worried he was asking too much of her despite her assurance the extra work kept her from missing her son so much.

He meant to only take a lap around the perimeter of the hanger to clear his head, but restlessness kept his feet moving. He sidled up to the aircraft and peered into the wheel well. "What's up with Yankee Nine?" he asked, referring to the unique identification number painted on the tail.

Fred Thomas turned from his work. "Mad said the hydraulic pumps were chattering."

Connor nodded but didn't question the mechanic further. With over forty years experience, the guy knew his craft better than anyone he'd ever met. Connor did wonder how much longer until Fred announced his retirement, especially considering how much overtime he'd been pulling down. "Did you tell Jeremy and Stan we needed them full-time?" he asked, referring to a couple mechanics he tapped for work on ad hoc basics.

"Sure did," Fred said, turning back to his work. "Made their day."

It looked like everyone was in a good mood except him. He patted the fuselage. He itched to get behind the yolk. Thank God, he was scheduled to take a couple businessmen over to Baton Rouge tomorrow.

"Here you are," Hillary said, ducking under the wing. "I need you to sign some checks so I can get them in today's mail."

He groaned just thinking about getting trapped in the office for the rest of the day. "I thought you said paying bills was more fun when there was money in the accounts." He joked as much to lighten his own mood as to tease his admin. It didn't matter how long he ran Aviation Options, sitting behind a desk would never be anything but a necessary evil. "I'm coming," he told Hillary before turning back to Fred. "I'll let you get back to work." Duty was a demanding mistress.

An hour later, he peeled off the glasses he now had to use when he worked at the computer and scrubbed his burning eyes with the heel of his palm. Sure, staring at a spreadsheet filled with black numbers instead of red was easier on the ulcer—but not for his head. It pounded like little gremlins were stabbing him with ice picks. He reached into his desk drawer for a packet of powdered pain reliever and downed it with the dregs resting at the bottom of a coffee mug. The cocktail of cold java and the bitter aspirin made him shiver as it slid down his throat.

The need to escape clawed at him. Maybe he'd take *The Nemesis* out this weekend now that she'd been repaired. The image of Avery sunning herself topside flashed in his head and he quickly dismissed the plan. Too soon.

"Not only did Inland Seafood's check come in, Avery got the Carolina Entertainment people to pay on time," Hillary said, pointing to the computer screen with a bright red fingernail.

He spared a moment to wonder what tactics she'd used to extract payment. Some larger corporations like Carolina Entertainment were notorious for paying sixty to ninety days late. Hiring her was the smartest thing he'd done in longer than he cared to admit. His heart ached at the unevenness of the scales. All he'd done in return was to cause havoc in her life.

Maybe once he returned from his flight to Baton Rouge, he'd treat her to dinner as a thank you. Even as he mulled over the idea he knew it was a no go. As her boss, he wouldn't do anything that might be construed as a come on. He wouldn't put her in that position no matter how much he still loved her. With the exception of her graciously befriending Sofia, he had to keep their professional and personal lives as separate as possible.

"So are we good to purchase those new laptops?" he asked, redirecting his thoughts.

"Absolutely," Hillary said. Her broad smile softened. "You were right to hire Avery. She's everything you said she'd be."

He nodded. *And more.* "I'm glad you think so." He checked the top of his desk, seeing he'd signed all the checks and approved all the accounts payable. "If we're done here, could you send Avery in? I want to ask how her flight to Raleigh went."

Hillary gathered the papers, shaking her head. "Unless she's walked in the door in the last few minutes, she's not back from the courthouse."

He checked his watch. "It's after two."

She eyed him meaningfully. "That can't be good."

Avery said it shouldn't last more than an hour, but clearly things weren't going as expected. She was also up against not just an ex-husband, but his entire clan. With no one for back up. He pushed back from the desk, the pledge he'd made moments ago getting trampled on his way out the door. "I'm headed downtown," he said, wondering what strings the Gaffneys pulled to fast-track the custody case.

"How long will you be?" Hillary asked.

"As long as it takes."

****

Avery cupped her hands together underneath the faucet of the bathroom sink then tipped the cold water into her mouth. Without a toothbrush, it was the best she could do to wash the taste of bile from her mouth. Then she took a second to wet a paper towel and cleaned up the mascara she'd smudged while she'd been reliving her lunch. The only thing that frightened her more than having her turn on the witness stand was the thought of losing custody of Will. Just contemplating the possibility sent her running for the ladies room. "You look like hell," she muttered under her breath and with that word of encouragement, she stepped into one of the courthouse's back hallways.

Michael Dougin, her attorney, approached. "Leave all the worrying to me," he said, patting her lightly on the shoulder. "That's what you pay me to do." Then he held the door open for her, and the two of them entered the courtroom.

That was easy for him to say. This day had kept her awake at night for weeks, especially after learning Rob's reason for bringing the case. She passed her ex-husband, without sparing him more than a glance and took her place across the aisle from him. Dressed in a suit and tie and with his hair slicked back, he looked every bit the young, earnest politician he proclaimed in his campaign posters. They didn't have long to wait before the bailiff called them to order and Avery was called to the stand.

Her hand trembled as she raised her right hand and swore to tell the truth: the whole truth and nothing but the truth. So help her God. Then she took the witness stand to the left of the Honorable Hamilton W. Boatwright—Ham to his drinking buddies and "sir" to everyone else in the county, his family included.

During the few times she'd accompanied Rob back to his hometown, she learned while much of the South had progressed into the new millennium, in Polk County in general and in Judge Boatwright's courtroom specifically, old times there were not forgotten. What could have easily been handled in one of the attorney's conferences rooms, or in chambers, was instead held in the turn-of-the-previous-century courtroom.

Rob's testimony had taken nearly two hours, with both his attorney and hers taking their respective turns. Dougin did a good job painting Rob as the perpetual Peter Pan that he was, but she didn't hold out hope this would be a quick and painless hearing which ended with the judge ruling in her favor. A person's name meant a great deal in this part of the country and her ex had done a good bit of reputation repair in the past year. According to Hillary, he and the incumbent congressman were tied in the polls.

As Avery settled into the wooden seat, she made eye contact with the only other woman in the room, Jessica Gaffney-Mims, Rob's attorney. *Damn, you* couldn't shake a stick without hitting one of Rob's kin. Avery schooled her features and waited for the opening bell.

"For the record, Ms. Madigan, please state your place of employment."

"I'm the Director of Sales and Marketing at Aviation Options," she said, her attention suddenly diverted to the back of the courtroom. *Well, speak of the devil.* Connor nodded in her direction then eased in the back row. Instead of unnerving her as he frequently did at work, his presence leant her a measure of peace. She needed a friendly face in this room, and his handsome one would do nicely.

"How long have you been employed there?"

"Four weeks, give or take a day or two."

The woman nodded as if that was something significant. "Before that where were you employed?"

"Flight Innovations in Atlanta," she answered, and

then tacked on, "for eighteen months."

"Are you also in the armed services?"

She and her attorney had previewed the questions she'd likely be asked and covered the possible reason for certain lines of questioning. What hadn't been discussed was a nugget of information she'd discovered on her own. It seemed while Judge Boatwright liked his poker games heavily liquored, and his clerks cute and female, he was also a veteran of Vietnam who generously supported the local VFW. While she didn't think her military service would be the deciding factor, it was worth at least some weight. "I'm a lieutenant commander in the Naval Reserves and served two tours in the Gulf," she said, aiming her answer directly at the judge who arched his considerable eyebrows in response.

"Thank you for your service," Ms. Mims quickly added, also noting the judge's reaction.

While the woman consulted her notes, Avery chanced a glance at Connor. His approval of her tactic radiated from the back row. As a habit, she didn't mention her career in the navy, not wanting to risk seeming to play on people's emotions. When it came to fighting for her son, anything was fair game.

Ms. Mims took a step closer. "How many times have you relocated in the past ten years?"

She took a moment to count all her relocations. To move up in the ranks, meant transferring often. Before Will, she'd been ambitious. "There were five."

"So your career requires you to move around a good bit," the opposing attorney suggested.

Avery cocked an eyebrow. "I've done whatever it took to provide for my son."

The woman tapped a pencil to her lips. "Does that also include nurturing and caring for the child you share with my client? Weren't you in fact absent a total of twenty-four months his short life?"

Avery's temper flared, and she bit the inside of her cheek to keep from firing off a smart-ass remark.

"Objection. Counsel is badgering the witness," her attorney finally chimed in.

"I'm simply laying the groundwork to show that my client would be the more stable parent given the amount of travel Ms. Madigan does," Ms. Mims countered.

While the two attorneys duked it out, Avery's mind rewound to her last deployment. Will had been a chubby-faced toddler when she'd left for the Gulf. Over the next twelve months she watched via video conference as he grew, learned new words, and began sleeping in a big boy bed. Not being able to tousle his hair or tuck him into bed each night killed her. Tears pricked the back of her eyes reliving those long, lonely days.

As a Super Hornet pilot, she'd been performing an important job that kept her country safe. Did men who served their country, risking their lives and sacrificing family time, have their parenting skills questioned, or was it only women who were expected to perfectly juggle career and home? It was wrong, but she'd grown to expect as much. Her attorney opened a can of worms digging into Rob's shenanigans and Ms. Mims some ground to make up.

"Overruled," the judge answered. "But tread lightly with any further questions, Ms. Mims."

Avery took a few deep breaths before she

answered. "I was gone when my service required it of me. I've since…"

"No further questions Your Honor," Ms. Mims said, cutting off the rest of Avery's response.

"I'd like to continue that line of questioning if I may, Your Honor," Dougin said.

Judge Boatwright nodded and Dougin stepped closer to the witness stand. "Are you on active duty now, Ms. Madigan?"

"No. I'm in the Reserves."

"So, you won't be deployed?"

She shook her head. While giving up her naval career hadn't been an ideal choice, it was a sacrifice she'd repeat in a pair of seconds. "Not in the foreseeable future."

With a nod Dougin retreated to his seat.

Ms. Mims sprang to her feet like someone struck a lit match to her ass. "Redirect, Your Honor," she said then sauntered over to the spot Dougin had just vacated. "You stated you didn't anticipate being deployed again." She jabbed a finger at Avery. "But in truth, you don't know that with absolute certainty."

Avery blew out a frustrated breath, feeling like a battered tin can caught between the two attorney's bantering. She looked to the back of the courtroom, latching onto Connor's presence for strength. Through a tight jaw he offered up a strained smile. "I don't have a crystal ball, so no, I don't know that it's impossible for me to be recalled to active duty, but I also don't know that I won't get cancer or be in a car accident."

Ms. Mims opened her mouth to once again cut off Avery's comments. But she had a head of steam and frankly didn't care if Judge Boatwright found her in contempt; she was getting her say. She locked onto Connor's gaze, hoping he knew how grateful she was for his help. "I do know this. I have a stable job here in LaGrange, and I've always done everything humanly possible to be a loving mother to him."

Several heartbeats of silence passed with everyone frozen in a tense tableau. Had she gone too far? Finally, Rob's attorney spoke, "No more questions, Your Honor."

Avery let out a breath and once she was released from the witness chair, walked on unsteady legs back to her spot next to Dougin. There was more legal maneuvering, then the moment of reckoning.

Judge Boatwright shuffled the papers before him. "In light of the testimony from both the plaintiff and the defendant, I'm ordering a home study be conducted on both households." His booming drawl echoed around the room and sent her pulse kicking into overdrive. She could live with having her home inspected. She'd pit her parenting and housekeeping skills against Rob and Tiffany's any day. But what about any temporary custody changes? The judge rambled on about a court-appointed guardian ad litem and time lines for her filing her findings with the court, but Avery yearned for him to get to the important part. Dougin had warned Judge Boatwright could make changes if he wished. She covered her mouth and took deep breaths, willing her stomach to settle.

"At this juncture, I'm disinclined to make changes to the custody arrangements. I order they stand as outlined in the divorce decree until I make my final ruling in one month."

Avery sagged in her chair, feeling like she'd been

given a reprieve—albeit a temporary one. As a measure of her tension eased, her thoughts turned to Connor. He'd been there for her even when she herself didn't realize how much a friendly face would mean. The moment Judge Boatwright brought the gavel down, she bolted from her chair. When she found the back row empty she kept moving, catching up to him in the lobby.

"Titan." He stopped in front of one of the fifteen-foot doors leading outside. "Thank you for being there." She took his hand, giving it a squeeze. "It meant a lot."

He tugged free of her grasp. "It was nothing. Just being a good boss."

Over the past weeks her anger toward him cooled. It hurt things ended as they had, but that didn't make her ungrateful. "That was way above the call of duty for a boss. You were being a good friend, and I appreciate it." Maybe they could actually *be* friends.

He shrugged. "I'll see you back at the office."

Then he pushed the door open and was gone. She fought hard against the urge to take off after him and was only saved from making a fool of herself when Dougin caught up to her. Clearly, Connor was more comfortable keeping this strictly professional.

Chapter Fourteen

Heat danced in waves off the concrete tarmac of Mobile Regional Airport. In a hurry to get out of the moisture-rich air, Avery hustled toward the small metal building just beyond the taxiway. She pushed open Wings 'N Thing's glass front door and breathed in the wonderfully air-conditioned air. She'd been flying since dawn, first delivering medical supplies to a hospital in south Georgia and then hauling machine parts to a company here in south Alabama. First on her agenda after checking in with the aviation servicing company was a bathroom break and something cold to drink. She leaned on the high counter and waited while the receptionist finished her call. "Yankee Nine needs refueling," Avery said. "How long do you think before you can get to me?"

The rawboned woman consulted her clipboard. "It'll be about an hour," she said, nodding to the waiting area where two uniformed men sat in front of a flat screen television. "Those two are ahead of you."

"No problem," Avery said before heading to the restroom. Afterward, she made a beeline for the drink machine and fed it a few coins then took one of the seats on the far side of the pilots' lounge. Once cargo was loaded and the ground crew topped off her plane, she'd make the return trip to LaGrange—where she'd spend another evening alone in her apartment streaming movies until she fell asleep on the sofa. Until Will returned from Steph and Opie's, their apartment would feel more like a storage facility than a home.

She popped open the top of her drink and made a mental list of tasks she still needed to do before the court representative came next week. With plenty of time in the evenings for cleaning and organizing her apartment, the only thing she could come up with was buying a new bathmat for the tub. Her stomach still twisted at the idea her parenting skills were up for review. Her only comfort was the fact Rob had to pass the same inspection.

Avery pulled her e-reader from her flight bag and tried to tune out the noise from the nearby flat screen where the two men were watching a game show. A few page-turns later, the excited voice of one of the men cut through her Tom Clancy thriller.

"Damn, and I thought I was having a bad day."

"Man, I bet that hurt," the other added. "You reckon the pilot walked away?"

Avery lowered the screen enough to catch a glimpse of a small jet nose first into the grass. She'd been lucky in her career never to experience anything more than a few rough carrier landings, unlike the unfortunate soul whose wrecked aircraft filled the TV screen. She credited her flawless record to skill and caution, but in truth sometimes things happened that no amount of planning could avoid. Curiosity and professional sympathy had her moving closer to the television.

A woman dressed in a bright pink suit, mile-high heels, and sporting a two-story hairdo stood in the foreground. "The NTSB and airport authorities have declined to comment on the cause of the crash or disclosed the condition of either the pilot or passengers," she said. "We'll bring you up to date as new information becomes available. This is Pamela June Henderson, Channel Four Action News reporting from Baton Rouge Metropolitan Airport."

Fear stole Avery's breath. Earlier in the day, Connor had left to deliver a couple businessmen to that Louisiana city. *God, please don't let that be his plane.* She tried to reason with the anxiety dancing up her spine. Dozens if not hundreds of planes took off and landed at that regional airport. Besides, while he might be a bit more reckless than she, he also had the skills to back it up.

"What do you think caused it?" the first pilot asked.

His companion shrugged. "This time of year my money's on a thunderstorm."

"No," Pilot One said, shaking his head. "I'm calling it as hydraulic failure. Did you see the way the nose gear collapsed?"

"That happened to me about five years ago," Pilot Two responded.

"Yeah, did you need a change of underwear afterward?" his buddy asked with a laugh.

Avery tuned out their banter, finding their gallows humor sickening. Instead, she focused on pleading with the Almighty that the unfortunate pilot be someone other than Connor. After the commercial break ended, she willed the reporter to return. What she needed was information, some solid facts that would push the elephant sitting on her chest. Instead, some guy— probably a former hometown athlete-turned-newscaster—rambled on about how the Texas Rangers were six games out of the lead in the AL West. As he prattled on and Pilots One and Two continued speculating about the crash, she bit the inside of her cheek to keep from screaming at all three men. She also talked herself out of calling Hillary—there was no sense in inflicting her overactive imagination on the other woman. Just because her life seemed to be swirling the bowl didn't mean she had to assume the worst.

Finally, Pamela June returned. While she repeated essentially the same tidbits of information, the camera panned to the upturned aircraft. Fire retardant foam covered the runway and much of the underbelly of the fuselage. Bile burned the back of Avery's throat as the plane's tail number came into view. 73WY8—Connor's plane.

Avery's vision darkened, her head swimming with the sudden influx of adrenaline. Her eyelids clenched for a moment. *Get it together*. She drew in a deep breath and forced herself to look at the scene objectively. Yankee Eight was intact. There wasn't a fire. It was a survivable crash. She scanned the background, hungry for a glimpse of Connor and when none came, she continued reasoning with her very unreasonable fear. He was likely holed up somewhere talking to airport officials, not in the back of an ambulance as her imagination insisted.

After snagging her phone she stepped out of earshot. Her hand shook as she punched in Hillary's number.

"I was just about to call you," the woman said instead of hello.

"Have you talked to him?" Avery asked, tears clogging her throat.

"No, but someone from the NTSB phoned. The guy said there were injuries, but couldn't tell me how bad they were." Emotion seemed to be getting the better of Hillary as well. Her voice climbed several octaves as she said, "Hang tight, Mad. I'll call you back when I hear more."

If she got any tighter, she'd never unwind. "Will do," she managed, when in reality she was ready to beg for a scrap of information. Or forget about the load of seafood she was supposed to pick up and head straight for Baton Rouge. For the moment it seemed better to stay put. After ending the call, she redirected her attention to the TV screen.

Her nails dug into her palms. He was probably rushing the landing and blew out a tire. Why did Connor always take risks? Didn't he know there were people who needed him? She folded her arms across her chest against the goose bumps dotting her arms. Didn't he realize there were people who loved him?

Slowly, anger overtook her fear. *Damn him,* she thought, more comfortable with being mad than experiencing the chill-inducing terror. She punched in Connor's cell number, not giving much thought what she'd say. It went immediately to voice mail. His cheerfully polite greeting stood in grave contrast to the situation. "Dammit, Titan, you better not be dead," she growled before hanging up. Tears threatened again. She'd be lost without him. Seconds later when his ringtone sounded, she nearly dropped the phone trying to answer it.

"It'll take more than a bird strike to do me in," he

said, with a laugh that was probably meant to be more light-hearted that it actually sounded.

"Are you hurt?" she choked out. As relief flooded her system, she gripped the edge of her chair for support.

"Just a gash over my eyebrow and a killer headache, but Yankee Eight will be out of commission for a while."

"Forget about the plane. It can be fixed," she quickly assured him. "I'll be down to get you as soon as my cargo gets unloaded and I file a new flight plan."

"You don't have to do that. Finish your route. I'll catch a commercial flight back home."

She gritted her teeth. "Don't argue with me. I'll be there in two hours." Didn't he see she needed to lay eyes on him? Everything changed in the moments she hadn't known if he was alive or dead. She might have still lost him as a lover, and he would probably always make her want to bang her head against a brick wall, but at least he was around to drive her crazy.

Her emotions swung like one of those Flying Dutchman rides at a carnival. When she got her hands on him, she didn't know whether she'd deck him for scaring her like that, or hug him tightly and never let go.

****

Once Avery got her plane back in the air, it took every ounce of self-control to rein in her anxiety. She opened the throttle, making the short hop between the two cities in quick time. Unlike her usual by-the-numbers landing, she came in hot and heavy, hitting the deck hard. Her stomach twisted as she rolled past the wreckage. She could see sky through the center of the jet engine where the blades should have been. It must have been a damned pterodactyl to do that much damage.

After parking the plane, she headed straight for the Airport Authority building. She spied Connor through a glass door, his back to her as he stood surrounded by a cluster of men. She practically yanked the doors off their hinges to get to him. His face jerked in her direction, revealing a large bandage on his forehead and a face lined with worry. She plowed through the group, not slowing to think through her actions. Her arms came around his waist and she pressed her face into his chest. The acrid scent of jet fuel mixed with his aftershave brought tears of relief to her eyes.

After a moment he returned her embrace, rubbing gentle circles over her back. She could have sworn he pressed his lips to her hair, but that was likely her imagination hard at work. Her heart aching, she would have been content to hold him until she'd convinced herself he really was safe, but an uncomfortable cough from one of the other men drove them apart.

"Hi," Connor said when she finally let him go. "Thanks for the ride."

****

Twenty-four hours after the accident, Connor shifted uncomfortably in his office chair, trying to find a position that didn't make him hurt like a son of a bitch. The aches had really set up shop, making him feel ninety-two instead of thirty-two. He groaned, as the movement seemed to aggravate the pain instead of alleviating it.

"Can I get you something for the pain?" Hillary asked, poised in her seat across from him. His admin had been hovering all morning.

"I'm on it," Sofia responded, bounding out of her seat and sprinting out of the room.

"You shouldn't even be here," Avery said, adding her opinion to the mother hen treatment he was getting. Worry lines furrowed her brow. "All this can wait until you're feeling better." She reached across the desk to touch his hand, the first pleasant sensation he'd had since her embrace yesterday.

As much as he wished he could take the day off, there were too many fires to put out. "Actually, no it can't." Besides dealing with the NTSB who'd already hit him up with more questions, he'd fielded calls from two clients and the fueling company that he owed four figures to. Then there were the forms the insurance company needed. God, it would be months before that claim was paid out. The walls seemed to be closing in, igniting his fight-or-flight instincts. For a fleeting moment, he gave serious consideration to loading Sofia on his boat and skipping town. One look at Avery, and that fantasy evaporated. Instead, it looked like he'd be sacrificing *The Nemesis* on the altar of good sense.

"Well, at least let me take a couple things off your plate," Avery said. "I'm sure I can convince everyone despite being a plane down, we'll still be able to honor our contracts."

He wasn't so sure about that. He clinched his fist in frustration. Just as Aviation Options got its head above water, shit hit the fan. He chuckled darkly at the irony. He'd been flying Yankee Eight in perfectly smooth air when out of nowhere a big ass bird had gone all kamikaze, destroying the jet engine's blades. He still couldn't get his mind around how one second he'd been talking to air traffic control and the next he was fighting to keep the plane aloft. "You know Yankee Eight is probably totaled," he said, to give her a reality check. There'd be no easy fixes this go-round.

She nodded, her eyes filled with pity. "I figured as much. But working when you're obviously in pain doesn't help." She gave his hand another squeeze. "Please, Connor, you've got a concussion. You've got to take care of yourself."

If he was looking out for Number One, the last thing he'd do was take a pain reliever and call it a day. He'd be doing whatever it took to get the woman he loved back. Unfortunately, doing what he wanted and what was right were polar opposites—which was why he needed to keep her at arm's length. "I'm fine." Besides, he didn't want anyone's pity no matter how much he was in love with her. "I don't need you smothering me."

She flinched. Hurt darkened her face before she schooled her lovely features. "I'll leave you to it then," she said, standing to leave.

He let her go. It was better this way. He needed to keep his distance despite what his body—and his heart insisted. For those precious few seconds yesterday when she'd wrapped her arms around him, he'd let himself believe there was more to her actions than worry. Even if that were true, with him as her boss he couldn't act on those feelings.

"I'm going to say that's the concussion talking," Hillary said, shooting him a look. "You got to know she cares about you, despite you being an ass." She stood then collected her files from the corner of his desk. "We all do."

"Yeah, well, that's not paying the bills now, is it," he said to her retreating back. He shook his head, refocusing on the crisis he could fix and not the disaster he couldn't. Reaching for the phone, he locked down his emotions. "Bash," he said when his former navy buddy picked up. "You still interested in buying my boat?"

****

A week after the crash, Avery took her first few tentative steps onto the marina's boardwalk. Hesitation weighted her steps not only because it was the first time she'd been near the water since that fateful day when she swam to shore, but for the fear Connor might not appreciate her presence. She learned through Hillary how he planned to get the money to replace the plane he lost. Though it made sense to her from a logical standpoint, and she'd certainly never seen the appeal of a floating death trap, he loved *The Nemesis*.

Weeks ago when she thought he'd cheated her out of the Carolina Entertainment contract, she said Connor would stop at nothing to succeed. Now as she drew closer to his yacht, she mentally modified that statement. There wasn't anything he wouldn't do to take care of the people he loved.

Standing on the dock, her pulse ticked up a notch. Things had been weird between them in the last few days—even more awkward than the detente they'd worked out at the beginning. It had to be the hug she'd given him. It had been pure impulse, but she couldn't bring herself to regret it even if it only intensified her longing for him instead of sating the loneliness. For those few seconds at least something was as it should be.

"Permission to come aboard, Captain," she called out.

A few seconds ticked by before Connor's shock of dark hair came up from below deck.

"Avery," he said, taking the few steps to the boat's railing. "Is everything okay with Sofia?"

She should have anticipated his response. He worried more about that girl than a hen with her chicks. "She's fine. I dropped her and Meghan back at Emma's house, so they're good for the night." As promised, Avery had taken the girls to a nail salon and then to see the latest teen flick in lieu of the birthday party.

"Oh, okay," he said still staring at her.

"Can I come aboard?" she asked, more certain she'd made a mistake in coming. On the way home from dropping off the girls, she thought he might like some company. He'd been through as much in the past weeks as she had.

"Yeah, sure. Sorry," he muttered. He held out a hand for her to step across the gap between the dock and the boat.

The contact zinged up her arm. It was the first time since becoming his employee he'd voluntarily touched her. She wanted to hold on to his hand a little longer, but didn't. Her visit wasn't about easing her need, even though she craved the feel of his hard muscles against her skin and his lips on hers.

"Did you need something?" he asked, his brow furrowed. "I know you don't like the water."

"Hillary told me you were selling the boat to Bash. I thought you might like some help getting things squared away." His look of puzzlement had her tacking on, "That's the kind of thing friends do, right?"

His fists clinched at his side. Had that been a huge assumption on her part? Not until that moment had she paused to consider he might simply see her as another person to be responsible for. His dark gaze raked over her. "We are friends, aren't we?" she asked. She'd been so quick to take on the role of injured party, she hadn't considered all the ways she'd wronged him by questioning his motives.

"Yeah," he said.

Not a resounding endorsement, but she took a couple steps toward the center of the boat all the same. She pointed below deck. "Do you have any personal stuff you want me to carry up to your car? Or I can clean the galley if you need."

"I've got it. I've been here a couple hours, so everything's pretty much good to go. I'm just waiting for Bash so I can hand over the keys and show him a few things." He crossed his arms over his body. "I've been meaning to ask, how'd the home study go?"

"It went fine." It had gone off without incident, unlike her attempts now. She eased onto the cushioned seat ringing the outside of the boat. "I guess instead of offering to help, I need to offer you an apology."

She laced her fingers together in her lap, searching for the right words. "I've jumped to a lot of conclusions lately. I shouldn't have assumed the worst of you." When he didn't say anything, she tacked on. "I should have given you a chance to explain. I also hoped maybe we could…" Her words trailed off. Getting friend zoned was a long way from where she'd once been. She'd take his friendship if that was all he had to offer. Another one of her assumptions—that he'd forgive her. His jaw ticked as she wound down her not nearly enough apology. "I'll get out of your way," she said turning for the dock. Tears stung her eyes.

He touched her shoulder, stopping her from leaving. "Wait." His lips pressed together in a straight line. "We're good, Mad." He trailed his other hand up her arm, sending licks of desire burning through her veins. "It's just…" He looked over his shoulder toward the banquette—the place where they'd made love.

Was he remembering it, too? If he was, did he look back on that time with longing as she did, or with regret?

"You caught me off guard, that's all."

She studied his blue eyes, the corners creased with too much sun and worry. She cupped the back of his head, wanting to pull him down for a kiss. His tongue wetted his lips. He leaned in.

The thud of footfalls against the wooden dock broke the spell. He jerked away from her, putting the width of the boat between them. "Bash," he called, laughing a little too loudly. "I was beginning to think you were backing out."

"I stopped off at a sporting goods store for some supplies," he said, holding up two armloads of plastic bags." His gaze darted between them. "I wasn't sure what you were leaving." His easy smile faded. "Everything all right, Mad? Rob and Tiff giving you grief?"

For once her legal issues with her ex weren't the most pressing problem. "No," she said, urgently needing to escape. "I was just leaving." She patted Bash's shoulder then climbed over the boat's rail. "Take good care of *The Nemesis*. She's a yare ship."

Avery left the two men without looking back or

acknowledging their good-byes. Their gazes pressed into her back as she walked toward her car. Confusion and desire swirled in her brain, clouding her thoughts. In the moments before Bash's arrival, she'd sworn Connor's feelings matched her own. He was going to kiss her, and if he had, things wouldn't have stopped there. A question muscled through the imagery her imagination conjured. Not whether she'd have let him make love to her—no doubt about that. Was it possible for them to regain what they'd lost?

****

Connor's gaze trailed after Avery. He rubbed the back of his neck, where the memory of her touch still burned. Thank God Bash arrived when he did. Otherwise, who knew what he'd have done. *Scratch that.* He'd been two seconds from kissing her, and if he had, there'd have been no stopping him. As much as his body screamed for the feel of her skin, to be buried in her tight heat, he wouldn't give in to those desires. That ship had not only sailed, but was way over the horizon. Her needs came first, and right now she needed a secure job with a boss who kept things professional.

"Let's do this," he said, focusing on a problem he could fix. Once he deposited Bash's check, Aviation Options' finances would be back on track.

"What's doing between you and Mad?"

"She came down to help me move my gear off the boat," he said, hoping to throw his buddy off the scent by playing things cool. With any luck, excitement about his new purchase kept him from picking up on the tension arcing between Mad and him.

Bash rolled his eyes. "I'm throwing the bullshit flag on that statement. Something's going on, and it's not you guys' usual hate-fest."

Connor shrugged. "I haven't got a clue what you're talking about." He wanted to share about as much as he wanted a root canal. "So, are we doing this or not?"

"Sure, if that's how you want to play it," he said, reaching in his back pocket. "I've got the check right here."

Connor took the slip of paper. Seeing the zeros didn't bring quite the relief he'd hoped. His thoughts turned to his old man, who'd gifted him with the boat as a graduation/you're-not-wanted-here present. In life, Stephen Jacob St. James Sr. had never had a positive thing to say about his second son no matter how hard Connor worked to earn his father's approval. When he took over the family business, his dad refused to acknowledge either the dire condition the Golden Boy had placed the company in—or Connor's efforts to rescue it from bankruptcy. Until the day his dad died, he would have gladly traded the boat for an "atta-boy".

What was worse—wanting something he'd never had and never would? His thoughts swung back to the disaster that was his relationship with Avery. Or was wanting something he'd had and lost the heaviest burden he'd tote around for the rest of his days? "Thanks for getting me out of this bind," he said, pulling his thoughts out of the tailspin and pocketing the check.

"Hey, man," Bash said, gripping his shoulder. "I get you not wanting to part with your baby. She's a beautiful boat. I'd be glad to float you a loan instead."

He shook his head. As he'd been clearing his things out below deck, he'd come to the realization *The Nemesis* had lost much of her appeal. Sure she was still a dream to sail, but it would never be the same. The whole time he'd been packing up the dishes and stripping the sheets of the berth, he remembered his time with Avery. His gaze darted to the seating at the boat's stern. He'd never be able to look at those blue and white cushions and not see her spread out for him there. Her stamp was on everything she touched—including him. "It's time I gave into reality. My future includes paperwork and meetings, not the open seas."

"Does it include Mad?" Bash asked, his eyebrow arched.

"Sure," he said, feigning nonchalance. "She's been a huge asset to the company."

"That's not what I mean."

It was time to shut this conversation down. Both the one he was carrying on in his head and the sharing session his buddy seemed intent on. "I don't know what you're talking about."

"It's me here," Bash said, crossing his arms. "I've seen how you two are with each other. You both have got it bad."

Was he that transparent? He hoped Avery hadn't picked up on it. Again rubbing the back of his neck where she'd last touched him, he told Bash, "It doesn't matter how I feel about her."

The guy shrugged. "Maybe, maybe not."

Frustration twisted his gut. "You want to give some airtime to your love life? If you're expecting me to spill my guts, I expect reciprocity."

Bash held his hands up in surrender. "Oh, hell, no. There isn't anything but ugly to look at there."

"All righty then, what you say we salute *The Nemesis* with a couple beers. I've got some cold ones down in the galley."

The last thing Avery needed to worry about was her boss blurring the personal/professional lines. He vowed to himself to keep his distance from now on. Come Monday, he'd sit her down and make her see it might not even be a good idea for them to try the friendship thing. The thoughts of shutting her down left him cold.

Chapter Fifteen

Hours after leaving the marina, Avery still couldn't get her mind to turn off. In frustration, she tossed aside the book she'd been trying to read. Usually, she could lose herself in a good story, turning off the drama of her own life in favor of the ones plaguing the fictional characters. Tonight, she couldn't get the voices in her head to shut up. Between the primary election on Tuesday when the citizens of the area would decide if Rob should represent them in Congress and the hearing later in the week when the judge would rule if her ex won full custody of Will, her mind swarmed like a hornets' nest of worries. Then there was the debacle with Connor to keep her mind humming. She crawled out of bed, figuring if she wasn't sleeping, at least she could be productive. After setting up the ironing board in the living room, she slid a movie in her old DVD player and started in on her clothes for the week ahead.

Midway through the first blouse, a knock on her door cut through the opening music of *Top Gun*. She bit back a yelp at the unexpected intrusion. Her eyes darted to the clock on the DVD player. Nothing good knocked at one o'clock in the morning. She looked through the peephole and in a flash had the chain off the door.

"Sofia, what are you doing here?" she asked.

After scanning the hallway for the two other girls she'd spent the afternoon getting to know, Avery drew the girl inside. "Where are Meghan and Emma?"

Connor's niece had changed from the shorts and T-shirt she'd worn to the movies, now a red-sequined dress clung to her body like a second skin. Black eyeliner streaked down her face and twigs clung to her messy hair. "I don't know. When the cops came, we ran in separate directions."

"You better explain," Avery said, steering the girl to the sofa. Although going on those few words and the girl's appearance, she was beginning to form a pretty good picture all on her own. She fetched a glass of water and a couple wet paper towels from the kitchen, and then sat on the coffee table to listen to Sofia's explanation.

With a shaking hand, the girl lifted the glass to her lips. "We planned all along to go to Alexia Gaffney's birthday party. We used the sleep over at Emma's as a decoy. Her parents thought we were at Meghan's, and the Barnes thought we were at my house."

Avery's temper flared. "I can't believe you lied to me. To your uncle."

Sofia's shoulders slumped. "It was the party of the year. I had to go. It started out great. There was food and good music. Then some of the kids decided to go skinny dipping in Alexia's pool."

While that was bad enough, Avery's instinct insisted there was more to this story. "There was alcohol there as well, wasn't there?"

She nodded. "And pot." Her head jerked up, looking Avery in the eye. "I didn't smoke any or drink. The three of us just hung out dancing mostly. Then this guy…" She shook her head as if trying to break free from the memory. "He grabbed my hand and started dancing with me. Jeremy's really cute, and I liked that he was paying attention to me. After a couple dances, he wanted to go into the media room where some of the other kids were making out."

"Did he touch you?" Avery asked, her voice deadly calm. Her anger switched focus, and a mother-bear urge to hunt down a certain teenaged boy overtook her.

"He kissed me really hard, ramming his tongue in my mouth." Tears streamed down her face. "I didn't like it and started pushing against him. He wouldn't let go." She drew in a deep breath. "That's when someone yelled that the cops were there. Kids started running in all directions."

Avery rubbed at the twitch forming between her brows. God, the girl had been in so much danger and didn't even realize it. The police showing up had probably saved Sofia from being raped. "What happened to Emma and Meghan?"

Sofia dashed the tears from her cheek. "I couldn't find them. There were kids running all over the place, so when I saw someone crawl through the basement windows, I followed." She drew in a shuttering breath. "I couldn't show up at either of my friends' houses, and I certainly couldn't go back home. Uncle Connor always turns on the alarm system at night, and I'd never be able to sneak back into my room without him finding out." Sofia met her gaze. "I came here because I knew you would help me."

Avery drew the girl in for a hug. "I'm so glad you did." She pointed to Sofia's purse. "Let's see if we can get Meghan and Emma on the phone to make sure they're okay. Then you need to call your uncle."

Sofia's eyes widened. "I can't do that. He'll kill

me."

"No, he won't," she responded, shaking her head. Although it would be a long time before he let her out of his sight. She wouldn't help Sofia continue to lie to her uncle, though. "You have to tell him."

Sofia snagged Avery's hand. "Please. Let me spend the night here, and in the morning I'll go back home when he's expecting me."

"That's not happening," she said, stabbing a finger in the girl's direction. "And I don't appreciate you putting me in this position either. I went to bat for you over this little girls' day and you took advantage of me."

Sofia dropped her chin, nodding.

Avery's heart softened. The girl had been through enough for one night. The least she could do was run a little interference. "If you want, I'll call Connor to explain, and if he's okay with it, you can spend the night."

"Would you?" she asked, her red-rimmed eyes pleading.

She motioned to the phone again. "See if you can get Meghan and Emma, and I'll lay out some towels and a pair of my sweats in the bathroom for you. If he decides to come get you tonight, at least he won't see you looking like you're singing backup for Guns 'N Roses."

"Thank you, thank you, thank you," Sofia said, reaching for her phone. "I promise I'll never do another bad thing as long as I live."

Avery chuffed at the hastily made promise, then went to collect the change of clothes and place them in the bathroom. She returned in time to catch the phone conversation.

"I couldn't find you either. Is Emma with you?" There was a pause while the other girl answered. "Oh, God," she groaned. "Her parents will freak. Let me know if she calls. Yeah, me too. Bye." She let the phone drop to her lap. "Meghan made it to another of our friend's houses, but the cops caught Emma."

Avery bit her tongue to keep from reminding Sofia there were worse fates than the police taking Emma into custody. The girls led too sheltered a life to understand all that could have happened to them. She gestured toward the hall. "Go get cleaned up, and I'll make that call to your uncle." Her heart thudded as she punched in Connor's number. This would not be an easy conversation even under the best of circumstances.

It rang twice before he picked up. "Avery, what's wrong?" he asked, his voice gravelly with sleep.

She took a moment to appreciate her name on his lips. "It's Sofia. She's here with me. She's okay, but I need to tell you what happened."

"What! What do you mean, she's okay? Jeez, don't lead off with something like that," he barked, interrupting her explanation.

She plowed ahead. There just wasn't an easy way to tell someone their child lied to them and narrowly dodged catastrophe. "The girls snuck out and went to that Gaffney girl's birthday party. It seems you made the right call not giving her permission to attend. Some things went down, and the cops were called."

"What kind of things?" he roared. "Never mind, I'm coming over. I'll be there as soon as I can."

She could imagine the scene if he raced over here loaded for bear. While Sofia had certainly earned some serious punishment, the reaming out could wait. She'd been through enough for one night. "Why don't you let her stay the night? You can pick her up in the morning. I'll even keep watch to see she doesn't sneak out again."

He let out a breath. "You don't have to do that," he said, fatigue coloring his words. "She's not your responsibility."

"I know that." But she wanted to help. Between the plane crash and having to sell his boat, he'd been through a lot lately as well. "I'm glad to do it."

A heartbeat of silence passed. "Maybe it's for the best," he finally said. His voice bore the weight of more than this latest drama. "I'd probably go off on her and make things worse. She already feels like she can't come to me when she messes up."

Her heart ached for him. "Don't be too hard on yourself. We're all doing the best we can."

"I'll see you in the morning. Call me the minute she wakes up."

"Okay," she said and started to press the End button when his voice stopped her.

"Avery, thanks. You really are a good friend. I should have told you that earlier at the boat but didn't."

Her throat tightened. "You're welcome," she managed, then ended the call before she could make a confession or ask if there was a possibility there'd ever be more than friendship between them.

She took a few minutes to get Sofia situated in Will's room, repeating what Connor had said and assuring the girl once again that everything would look brighter in the morning.

Avery closed the bedroom door and returned to the

living room. The excitement of the past hour drained all her excess energy, so she unplugged the forgotten iron and put it, the ironing board, and the laundry basket away. She'd just retrieved her book from her bedside table and curled up on the sofa when another knock came on her door. This one didn't surprise her, and she didn't bother to check before opening it to Connor.

"I tried to wait, but I just couldn't do it."

He might not be her biological father, but no one could care more for a child. Given what happened in the girl's short life, her birth parents certainly hadn't. He looked like tortured hell. Dark circles shadowed his eyes and his hair stood on its ends like he'd used his fingers to comb it. Her fingers itched to rub across the stubble shadowing his jaw.

"I won't yell at her. I just need to see for myself she's okay."

"I'd feel the same way," she said, letting him inside. His gaze darted around her home. "I put her in Will's room." She pointed beyond the living room. "It's the first door on the left." Then she went into the kitchen to start the coffee brewing. She was reaching for the mugs when he found her.

"She's already asleep, so I didn't wake her," he said from behind. His warm scent wafted over to her.

"You want some coffee?" she asked, gripping the handle of the carafe so she wouldn't turn around and grab him instead.

"No, thanks, I should get out of your hair so you can get some sleep."

"Stay," she said, catching his hand before he could leave. "You know you want to."

His gaze darkened, and she quickly amended. "I

meant you won't be able to rest until you've gotten to talk things out with Sofia." She shrugged to cover her unease. "It'll be morning in a few hours, and you can hang out with me until she wakes up."

He nodded. "Only if it's not an imposition."

They moved to her living room, each settling on opposite ends of her sofa. The near darkness, rather than hiding their obvious unease, seemed to add to the heaviness between them. She clicked on the television and after flipping through the channels, stopped on a showing of *South Pacific*. She didn't care anything about watching the musical, but it beat the silence filling the room.

"You ever think about digging a moat around you and Will and pulling up the drawbridge?" he asked. His voice sounded not just tired, but defeated.

Avery couldn't do much to fix the sense of failure he had to be experiencing, but she could let him have some rest. She crossed the room to the bench where she kept a couple soft blankets. Returning, she handed one to him and answered. "Sometimes I do." Settling back on her side of the sofa, she curled her feet underneath her and tucked her own blanket around her body. "More often, my daydreams involve flights to far away countries that don't share an extradition treaty with the U.S."

"When does the judge make his decision?"

"Thanks to the Gaffney family's influence," she said. "The case got pushed to the front of the court docket. We're on the schedule for Friday." Never far from her mind, the full weight of the child custody suit descended on her.

Connor shifted to her side and put his arm around

her shoulder, sending a jolt of electricity through her body. "If things don't go your way—the way they should—I can help you make that happen."

Avery didn't doubt for a moment that he would. Tears of gratitude welled. She laced her fingers through his, giving his hand a squeeze. "Thanks, but I'm putting my faith in the judicial system." She'd never actually go through with the plan. It was simply an idea she conjured up to help her believe she had some control over the situation. "I probably shouldn't even joke about a thing like that."

"I've had my share of illogical pipedreams," he said, stroking her hair as he held her close. "More than once I've thought about chucking it all in and disappearing on my boat with Sofia."

Connor wasn't the only one entertaining fantasies. His gentle caresses stoked her desire. Lust pooled in her belly. Before good sense had a chance to weigh in, she crawled into his lap. Her mouth found his in a bruising kiss. After so long—all those weeks they'd been lost to each other—her need for him drove her beyond caution, or even self-preservation. Her fingers raked through his hair, pulling him in. When his arms snaked around her waist and he deepened the kiss, her heart soared. She hadn't mistaken those looks on the boat. He'd forgiven her, wanted more than friendship.

She feathered kisses across his cheek. "Stay," she murmured, and then nibbled his earlobe. "Make love to me. I've missed this so much. Missed you."

He froze then bolted from the sofa, practically dumping her onto the floor. "No. I can't. I won't."

She scrambled to her feet in a feeble attempt to recoup some of her dignity. She needn't have bothered—it lay in tatters. But she hadn't been mistaken. She'd tasted his hunger, felt his erection hardening beneath her, and sensed his need. His words filtered through her embarrassment. "I don't understand."

He raked his hands through his hair, pulling on the ends. "It's not a matter of what I want. It's not right."

What was wrong about them being together? Before they'd made a mess of things, they'd talked about giving a relationship a try. "Give me a clue here. What's wrong with us being together if it's what we both want?"

"Can't you see? You work for me. I'd never do that to you."

He was clinging to rules that didn't apply anymore. "We aren't in the navy now, and there's no law that says we can't be together as long as it's mutually agreeable. It's not like there's a company policy against office romance." She arched an eyebrow "Is there?"

"It's never been an issue before." He rolled his eyes. "We both know I haven't had much regard for regulations. All the underhanded things you thought I'd done over the years, well, I'm guilty of all of them and then some. But in this one area I'm not crossing the line. I won't take advantage of you."

"But it's not a line if we both agree," she said reaching out to him.

He crossed his arms over his chest. "What would happen if things didn't work out?"

"We'd be adults about it," she said with a shrug. "We've managed okay since I came to work for you."

He barked out a laugh. "I'm not so sure how well we've managed." His eyes softened. "My gut tells me

Judge Boatwright will rule for joint custody. It's the right thing for Will to have both his parents in his life. If that's the case, you'll need to continue to work for me. I couldn't stand the thought that you'd feel you had to stay in a relationship with me to protect your job."

She opened her mouth to argue, but he touched a finger to her lips. "Leave me this one way in which I've been honorable."

She nodded then looked away so he wouldn't see the tears streaming down her cheeks.

"I'm going," he said. "Have Sofia call me when she wakes, and I'll come back for her."

"Sure," she managed through a throat thick with emotion.

Avery lasted about a second after he'd pulled the front door closed before melting into a full-blown crying jag. She leaned against the kitchen countertop for support. *Of all the rules for him to stick to.* At least when she'd first taken the job, she could hide behind her righteous anger. They'd reached an impasse. How would she face him in the morning, and every workday after, knowing he'd never budge despite how they both felt?

****

Days later, the printer next to Avery's desk hummed as it spit out a freshly negotiated contract. Between Rob's narrow election defeat, negotiating her most complicated contract to date, and today's custody hearing, she'd trade the commission check she'd earned for a quiet weekend—one where the court's ruling left Will in her custody.

She let out a breath and pushed back from her desk. Not that she begrudged Rob the opportunity to co-parent with her. Equal time with a predictable schedule was in their son's best interest. On the way to the printer, she passed Sofia at her desk. Quiet and compliant, the girl seemed resolved to the grounding her uncle had surely given her. By silent agreement, they didn't discuss any of that night's events.

Just as Avery returned to her desk, Connor burst in from the hangar. "Oh, good, you're still here," he said, loosening the tie he wore with his pilot's uniform.

Heat flooded her cheeks. Another thing that made the past week one for the books—having to pretend she was okay with sticking to his no fraternization rule. All the logic in the world couldn't convince her heart not to feel as it did. "The Palm Coast people sent this over," she said, handing him the contract. "I was just getting ready to put it on your desk."

He took it from her. "Great, but that's not what I meant. I wanted to be sure I got back in time to go to the courthouse with you."

Gratitude tightened her chest. His steadying presence weeks earlier had been a beacon in a sea of uncertainty. She hadn't let herself hope he'd do it again. After that night, a chasm deepened between them. Awkward and brief best described their few conversations. Her resolve to adhere to his wishes was strung as tightly as her nerves. Even now as she stood in front of him with Sofia and Hillary talking in the background, she wanted to reach for him. She crossed her arms to prevent herself from acting on the urge.

All the awkwardness aside, she needed someone there with her more than she needed to preserve the remnants of her pride. "Thank you," she breathed. "I'm leaving in a few minutes, so you can follow me over or meet me there if you're busy."

"I'll drive you."

Her eyes widened. The two of them hadn't been alone since that night—likely by his design and not happenstance. "I'll be ready in a second." Her mouth dry and her pulse pounding, she pulled her purse out of her desk drawer.

As she slung it over her shoulder, her phone vibrated inside. Her attorney was calling. "Mr. Dougin," she said, wondering what he could want at this late hour. They'd already gone over all the possible contingencies and their responses the day before. "I'm on my way to the courthouse right now."

"That won't be necessary," he said.

Crap! She couldn't take a continuance. Every day she had with her son was precious, but as much as she feared losing Will, she couldn't continue to live in this limbo. "Why? What happened?" Unease settled in her stomach.

"The case has been dropped."

"Do you mean Judge Boatwright dismissed Rob's petition?" she asked.

"No. Your ex-husband withdrew it. I just got off the phone with his attorney."

She cupped shaking fingers to her lips. Tears trickled down her cheeks. For the briefest second, gratitude toward Rob filled her. *But why?* "Did Ms. Mims say what prompted the change?"

"She didn't, but I have a theory if you're interested."

"Absolutely," she said. Not from curiosity, but because she needed to know if she could expect Rob to do this to her and Will the next time a parental whim overtook him.

"Tuesday he lost the primary election to the incumbent, and now he's out of the race he no longer needs to keep up the happy family façade."

Anger flared inside her. Despite knowing Rob was a Peter Pan with good acting skills—she'd held onto the belief he actually wanted to be a parent to their son. "That makes sense in a sick and twisted sort of way."

"It's just my guess, but anyway, I'm glad things worked out for you."

"Me too," she said, still trying to wrap her head around the sudden, wonderful change of events.

"What was that all about?" Connor asked when she'd ended the call.

"Rob dropped the case."

His reaction mirrored hers moments before: a brief smile followed by his eyes narrowing. "This is good news, right?" Then his smile returned. "This *is* good news. Let me take you to lunch to celebrate."

It took a moment for her to process his request. He was willing to be alone with her? Her head swam with the curve balls everyone kept throwing her way. "Okay," she said finally.

By the time they started the drive to Le Peeps, her questions began in earnest. Would Rob want to continue to see Will on alternating weekends as their divorce decree stated, or would he revert to his old ways of showing up in unpredictable intervals to shower their son with gifts and then disappear for months? With their homes less than five miles apart, she'd have to insist he call ahead before visiting. Will's life had been disrupted enough and the boy needed some stability.

Settling into the booth, she breathed in the comforting scent of coffee, buttermilk biscuits, and sausage gravy. Other than a lone diner at the back of the place, they had the restaurant to themselves. The knot in her stomach loosened a bit. This was exactly what she needed—a few quiet moments to get her head wrapped around Rob's sudden one-eighty. She and her son both needed to fly in some calm air.

Connor took a sip of the coffee their waitress had brought them, along with a couple menus. "I can't tell you how glad I am that Rob dropped the case, Mad. Though I'd totally have let you have one of my planes if things hadn't worked out."

She chuckled, relieved to finally close a particularly ugly chapter of her life. "Speaking of planes, how's the Beech Jet working out?" she asked, trying for a normal conversation.

He beamed. "Flies like a dream."

"But it's not as nice as *The Nemesis,*" she said, guessing his true feelings.

"Nothing's as great as she, but this way is more practical." He shrugged. "Face it, my dreams of sailing off into the sunset are just that—dreams. My place is here, nose to the grindstone and all that."

She respected the tough decisions he made as much as she wished he felt differently about the ones regarding their relationship. "Heavy rests the head that wears the crown, huh?"

"Something like that," he said, then flashed a broad smile. "What looks good? I'm feeling a celebratory burger is in order."

Her phone chiming in her purse cut off her response. She looked at the caller ID on the screen.

"Flight Innovations." She hesitated answering the call. The last person she wanted to hear from—other than Rob—was her old employer. She'd returned her company-issued laptop and left her forwarding address with HR. "Let me see what they want, then we'll get our celebratory lunch started." She pushed the Home key on her phone. "Madigan speaking."

"Ms. Madigan, this is Ed Rhodes from Flight Innovations. Do you have a moment?"

"Sure," she said. She'd always appreciated the VP's directness. He ran a tight ship and, with the exception of her former boss, didn't put up with anyone's bullshit.

"There have been some changes in our personnel, and Douglas Stanford is no longer with our company. I was calling to see if you'd be interested in taking his position."

Her heartbeat ticked up a notch. "You've caught me off guard, Mr. Rhodes." Talk about a day of unexpected hairpin turns. "I'm no longer in Atlanta. I've relocated to my new job."

"I'd heard, Ms. Madigan. I'm sorry you got away from us in the first place, and so I'm prepared to make you a generous offer which includes a moving package in order to get you to return."

Her pulse raced in earnest. If she returned to Flight Innovations, it would be like the past few months never happened. She looked across the table. Connor's jaw ticked as he stared at her, not even pretending to tune out her conversation.

The two of them needed to quit torturing each other. This look-but-don't-touch, love-but-don't-live situation wasn't good for either one of them. Something needed to change. If she returned to Atlanta, it would allow them both the peace they deserved. The words of acceptance perched on the edge of her lips. If she took the job, she could have Will back at his old school by the first day of class. She could even buy a house. Yet her lips wouldn't form the words. "Could I give you my answer on Monday? I'd like the weekend to think things over and talk to my son."

"Certainly, Ms. Madigan. I'm anxious to negotiate terms that will get you back. I don't mind saying you left quite the vacuum here."

"I'll call you Monday with my answer." She stowed her phone then picked up her menu as if she hadn't just been handed her dream job.

"Will you take it?" Connor asked. His dark gaze bored into her.

Avery laid the menu down. "I don't know," she murmured. Peering into the future, she could see only more of the same heartbreaking standoff if she stayed. "I need to think about it." Although what good would that do? Connor had made up his mind she was off limits. Frustration boiled inside her. She placed her napkin on the table, unable to stay hemmed into the booth another second. "Would you mind if I took the rest of the day off?"

"Sure, whatever," he said, standing then fishing a couple bills out of his wallet. "I'll drive you back to your car."

Chapter Sixteen

Hours later, Avery exited her car, smoothing her skirt as she crossed the parking lot. She'd timed her return to work well. Other than Connor's car, the lot was empty. Her hand trembled as she tugged the letter from her purse. Knowing she'd made the right decision wouldn't make the next few minutes any easier. She hurried to his office, rapping on his open door. "Got a minute?"

His face jerked in her direction and a look of resignation washed over him. "That didn't take long."

"I didn't see the point in prolonging the inevitable." She passed him the envelope and waited while he extracted the sheet of paper and read her letter.

"Effective immediately," he said, a pained look crossing his face.

She girded herself to get through the next few minutes. "Do you accept my resignation?"

"Of course," he growled, raking his fingers through his hair.

Her pulse pounded out a tattoo. "So, I'm no longer your employee, right?" she asked, coming around to his side of the desk.

He pounded the desk with his fist. "Jeez, Mad! I'm sure as hell not going to keep you here against your will."

"Just making sure before I do this," she said,

lowering herself to his lap. She twined her arms around his neck. "I wouldn't want you to break any of your self-imposed rules." Covering his mouth with hers, she first pressed teasing kisses to his lips, then gave into her desire by plundering the depths of his mouth. After a moment's hesitation, Connor got with the program. He fisted her hair, tearing it loose from its clip. Their tongues danced and tangled, fighting for domination.

When Connor broke the kiss, they were both breathless. He pressed his forehead to hers. "So is this good-bye?" he asked in a voice heavy with emotion.

"Not exactly," she said, hoping it was more like a new beginning.

His brow creased. "Do you want the job in Atlanta?"

"Not especially," she said with a shrug. "If that's what it takes to have a relationship with you, then that's what I'll do."

His face split into a broad grin. "What if I have a better idea?"

"I'm open to suggestions." Nearly anything would be better than enduring this torture.

Connor framed her face with this palms. "Stay?" The word was barely above a whisper.

She opened her mouth to argue but didn't get a chance to tell him how she couldn't take another day of keeping her hands off him.

"Let me explain." He smoothed down her hair that he'd mussed. "The company needs you." He pressed a kiss to her lips. "I need you."

Confusion washed over her. "What happened to your no fraternization with the employees rule?" His hands were everywhere—her face, shoulders, breasts.

This was definitely fraternization in the best possible way.

He reached in his desk drawer and pulled out a red box. "Marriage is a partnership of equals, correct?"

Her eyes widened. "Ideally," she squeaked out when she could finally find her voice.

Connor pushed the box in her direction. "If you marry me, then what's mine becomes yours."

Avery shook her head. "You make this sound like a business deal." She wanted love, passion, and forever—not a partnership with benefits.

He chuckled darkly. "When it comes to you, I'm all business." He picked up her hand, kissing each of her fingers. "Keeping you happy, safe, and well-loved is a full-time job." He shot her a heated look. "You know how seriously I take my job."

God! This was more than she'd hoped for. She reached for her resignation letter, intending to tear it into tiny pieces of confetti. Her plan to break their stalemate worked better than she'd imagined.

"Wait," he said, his hand closing over hers.

"What? I don't need to take the job in Atlanta now."

A wicked smile formed on his lips. "You can't undo the resignation."

She rolled her eyes. For a man whose reputation as a maverick reached mythic levels, he sure was a stickler for the rules. "Why?"

"Because I've been fantasizing about doing this for weeks now." Then bracketing her hips with his hands, he transferred her from his lap to the desktop. He brushed his thumb across her cheek, sending sparks of electric friction over her skin. "You haven't said 'yes' yet."

"What about our kids? Will hasn't even met you or Sofia."

His eyes grew tender. "I'll do whatever it takes to earn your son's affection." He pressed a gentle kiss to her lips. "As far as Sofia's concerned, she already thinks the world of you. I know she'll be excited to have Will in her life as well," he said, then brushed her hair from her face.

His touch clouded her thinking. Surely there were other things they needed to discuss. His hand trailed down her neck and shoulders. Avery gave herself over to the heady sensations, the warm scent of his aftershave, and the feel of his lips on her neck. Too consumed by desire, she could only nod. Cupping the back of her head, he brought his mouth to hers. Wanting more, she parted her lips and slipped her tongue into his mouth. Avery tangled her tongue with his, tasting a minty sweetness that did little to extinguish the building heat.

Then just as he dominated her thoughts, her heart, her world, he took over the kiss. Invading her mouth, he stroked her tongue into submission. She surrendered to the pleasure he brought, sinking deeper into his embrace. He knew exactly how to drive their kisses to a frenzy of lips, tongue, and teeth only to retreat and begin again.

Making a low, anguished growl, Connor pulled back and began to trail kisses across her jaw. "God, I want you," he breathed in her ear. He nipped her neck before soothing the tender flesh with his tongue. "I want to taste you."

"Yes," Avery whispered.

He slipped a hand between them to cup her breast. "I want to touch you."

"Yes," she pleaded, her nipples tightening with his touch.

He freed the buttons on her blouse, bearing her skin to the cool air and his heated stare. "I want to see you, Avery." Then he slid her top off her arms, letting it drift to the floor. "I want to see all of you."

"Yes." The air hissed out of her lungs. She wanted nothing separating them. She reveled in knowing he'd soon plunder her body, recalling the contours of his muscled shoulders and back as he arched above her, his scent as he became aroused, and the sounds he made as he climaxed.

Connor gently laid her against the hard surface of her desk, fanning her hair out behind her. "You look like an angel spread out like this—a fiercely beautiful angel."

Desperate to have him buried deep inside her, she fisted his shirt, trying to pull him on top of her.

A deep, erotic laugh escaped his lips. "And demanding." He purred into her ear. "Let me worship you the way angels deserve, Avery."

He eased back, leaving her feeling bereft. "No," she cried out. Beneath his weight, she felt grounded.

"Patience," he chuckled as he traced lazy circles around the lace of her bra. Connor tweaked each nipple in turn, grinning arrogantly as they hardened under his touch. With calloused fingers that abraded her skin, he tugged down the bra cups, pushing up her breast to his waiting mouth. As he suckled first one breast then the other, Avery combed her fingers through his hair, anchoring him in place. Every stroke of his tongue sent a zing straight to the apex of her thighs.

After pressing a tender kiss to each breast, Connor nibbled his way down her body. When he reached the curve of her waist, he drew down the side zipper and tugged her skirt partway down her hips. Then his hand trailed up from her knee. When he stopped at the edge of her skirt, so did her breathing. Slipping underneath, calloused fingers began hungrily edging their way up her thigh. They caressed the silk of her panties, teasing her mound.

His electric touch radiated to the very heart of her. "Mmmm," an aching need bubbled up from her core till it burst from her mouth as a throaty groan.

"You're so hot, so wet for me." Connor continued stroking her. His broad hands moved to her hips, pulling her to the edge of her desk. Then hooking her panties, he worked them slowly down her legs one excruciating inch at a time.

Avery blushed as he drew them to his nose and breathed in the scent of her arousal. "Like apples dipped in honey," he announced. Her eyes grew wide as he tucked them in his pocket.

"Do I get those back?" she asked.

His eyes darkened. "Not until you agree to marry me. I want to hear you say it."

"Okay, yes. I'll marry you." She groaned, dropping her head back to the desk in surrender.

"Finally," he said, then opened her further, exposing her most secret places, and lowered his mouth. His warm breath caressed her and at the first swipe of his tongue, she cried out. Between his fingers kneading the insides of her thighs, the stroke of his tongue, and the surge of electric energy, it was all too much. And yet it wasn't enough. Need ripped through her veins and she arched her back trying to bring more of her flesh into contact with his mouth.

With his palms against her hips he stilled her. "Slowly." Lifting his face to capture her eye, he murmured. "I want you to burn for me and when you're begging for release, I'll take you to heights of pleasure you've never known."

The sultry timbre of his voice was enough to have her begging, but then he lowered his mouth again and began keeping his promise. Avery felt herself spiraling higher, sensation and need coalescing into a torrent of energy. She flung her hands above her head in an attempt to latch onto something before she flew apart. He threaded their fingers together, and with that she peaked. An orgasm detonated in her core and radiated throughout her body. She trembled as the waves rocked through her and colors flashed before her eyes. Then everything became dark as she floated in a pleasure-soaked haze.

When she finally came back to her body, she found Connor watching her. "I can't wait to watch you do that for the rest of our lives," he said, a smug grin on his face. "I'm one lucky son-of-a-bitch." Awe colored his voice.

Heat pooled in her belly and she wanted, no she needed, more than just his hands against her skin or his mouth against her core. "Please…"

He looked at her, his blue eyes alight with lust. "Please what, Avery? Tell me what you want."

"You." She groaned. "I want you."

The corner of his mouth turned up in wicked grin. "You have me. Forever."

"Aaaah," she cried in frustration. He was torturing her, making her spell out what she wanted when she could barely string two words together much less describe all the decadent things she wanted him to do to her. She fisted his shirt, wanting to rip it and the rest of his clothes from his body. "Inside me, Connor. Now!"

"Now, later." He growled. "Here, and then again in my bed, I'll make you scream my name."

Avery reached for his belt, undoing the buckle with trembling hands. "I want more than my own pleasure," she murmured against lips that had found hers again. "I want to give you pleasure, to sate your longing, to touch your very soul till neither of us knows where one ends and the other begins."

At her words, Connor's blue eyes shot to hers. He froze, and she shifted her hand to his broad chest and stilled as he drew in deep breaths. "God, Avery, yes. That, that. That's what I've wanted for so long."

His tender words cooled some of her urgent sexual need. Their joining was more than meeting a physical imperative. Their souls belonged together, their lives and families entwined. If only they hadn't put each other through so much torture, they could have already spent years together. "We've wasted so much of our lives pretending to be enemies."

"Don't think like that," he said against her lips. "We'll just have to make up for lost time until we can no longer remember a time when we weren't together."

"Yes," she said, moving to join their bodies, even as his beautiful words had joined their lives.

Epilogue

Three months later

Avery drew in a deep breath and held it. "Now try," she said, praying she wouldn't have to resort to safety pins to hold her ivory wedding gown closed. The strapless dress fit snuggly to the hips where it flared elegantly to the floor.

Stephanie's brow knotted in determination, and she gave the zipper a hard tug. "That did the trick," her maid of honor said when it finally slid into place. "Another couple weeks and this wouldn't have fit."

"Shhh." Avery looked around the room to see if the others caught Steph's slip. "We don't want anyone to know just yet." She could hardly believe she was a week short of her second trimester. With Sofia and Hillary busy with their own preparations, she added in a whisper, "Connor and I will make the announcement when we get back from our honeymoon."

The weekend mountain getaway was more like a family vacation since both Will and Sofia would be joining them. That was fine with her. She touched her stomach which seemed to be growing by the day. As Connor predicted, their children took an immediate liking to each other. Her heart sang knowing they'd also welcome their new brother or sister. Happy tears pricked the backs of her eyes. They were on their way to being the family they all deserved.

Suddenly, Will burst into the room distracting her thoughts just as the tears were threatening to ruin her mascara. "Mommy," he said, rushing up to her. His tuxedo jacket, which matched Connor's and the other groomsmen, flapped behind him. "Uncle Connor wants me to give you this." He thrust a small box up at her. "He said it's important you have something new to wear."

"Thank you, sweetheart," she said taking the gift and kissing the top of his head.

Sofia put down her makeup brush and joined them. "What is it?" she asked, leaning in to see.

Her hands trembling, Avery untied the white ribbon and pried open the box. "Oh, my," she breathed as the silver bracelet caught the light. She fingered each charm—an airplane, boat, anchor, playing cards, and wine glass—dangled from the links. "Help me put it on," she said, her voice quaking. When had Connor gotten so sentimental?

Stephanie fastened the delicate chain to Avery's wrist then adjusted her veil. "You look perfect."

"She does, doesn't she," Sofia agreed. "Do we have time for a couple selfies? I promised Meghan and Emma I'd post some."

"Let me check my makeup one more time," Avery said, dabbing at the corners of her eyes.

"You look fine," Hillary said, joining them once she was free from the hairdresser. "Let's break into that sparkling cider before we head out," she said, the up-do and robin's egg blue bridesmaids dress complementing her fair completion.

A sharp rap on the door interrupted their revelry.

"Male on deck," Admiral Griffin said, peeking into the room. "Is everyone decent?"

"We're dressed, sir," she said, smiling as he looked sheepishly around the room dotted with women's clothes, makeup, and hair products. With the ceremony taking place at the naval air station's chapel, they'd commandeered one of the adjoining rooms to dress in.

"Avery, my dear, you make a stunning bride," he said, inspecting her from head to toe.

With both her parents deceased, she'd reached out to the man who'd been more father than mentor. "Thank you, sir," she said. She touched the sapphire broach Mrs. Griffin loaned her. "You giving me away means more than I can say."

The admiral cleared his throat then checked his watch. "It's time to go, ladies. We can't keep the groom waiting."

She tucked her arm in his with a smile. "They can't start this without me."

Moving to the vestibule, the *Wedding March* played on the other side of the chapel doors, kicking her pulse into overdrive. Then with a swish they were open, and her groom waited down at the altar for her. God, he was handsome dressed in a charcoal tux, his unruly hair trimmed neatly. She spared a brief glance at her friends, coworkers, and navy buddies as she stepped toward her future. For once, Connor's face didn't break into a wide grin when he saw her. If she hadn't known better, she'd have sworn those were tears turning his eyes a cobalt blue.

Admiral Griffin gave her away with a kiss on her cheek. Then Connor reached for her hand and they promised to love, honor, and cherish each other for the rest of their lives. With the last vows he wrapped his arms around her, kissing her long and hard to the delight of the congregation. Afterward they were off to the reception at the hotel where their adventure first began.

An hour later, they were midway through their first dance. "How soon can we leave?" Connor asked.

"What's the hurry?" For an event they'd thrown together in a matter of weeks, it was coming off nicely. Besides, they still had the toasts, the bouquet toss, and she was dying to talk to Hank and his sister, Mia, who came as his plus one. "We have the rest of our lives together."

Connor stilled them, cupping her face. His expression turned serious. "That's just it—I'm ready to start our forever."

She touched her belly, a smile playing at her lips. "Me too." Their romance was twenty years in the making, and that was plenty long enough to wait.

A word about the author…

Melissa Klein writes contemporary romance about everyday heroes fighting extraordinary battles. Whether facing the demands of caring for a child with special needs or the struggles of a soldier returning home, her characters take on the challenges life throws at them with perseverance, courage, and humor. She lives in Atlanta with her family and can be found online.

www.MelissaKleinRomance.com
https://www.facebook.com/Melissa.Klein.Romance

Thank you for purchasing
this publication of The Wild Rose Press, Inc.

If you enjoyed the story, we would appreciate your
letting others know by leaving a review.

For other wonderful stories,
please visit our on-line bookstore at
www.thewildrosepress.com.

For questions or more information
contact us at
info@thewildrosepress.com.

The Wild Rose Press, Inc.
www.thewildrosepress.com

Stay current with The Wild Rose Press, Inc.

Like us on Facebook

https://www.facebook.com/TheWildRosePress

And Follow us on Twitter
https://twitter.com/WildRosePress